D. M. FRASER

D. M. Fraser was born in Nova Scotia in 1946, grew up in coal-mining towns, and lived in Vancouver B.C. for most of his adult life. He took his B.A. at Acadia University, and did post-graduate work at the University of British Columbia. In the early seventies he left the academy and became involved with Pulp Press, the publishing house with which he maintained a close connection until his death in 1985. His first collection of stories, *Class Warfare*, appeared in 1974, and was followed by *The Voice of Emma Sachs* in 1983. Both books received unanimous critical acclaim. These books, his public readings, and his editorial work, made D. M. Fraser a legendary figure in Canadian letters. His untimely death in 1985 cut short his work on *Ignorant Armies*, which had been underway since the late seventies.

BRYAN CARSON

Bryan Carson and Don Fraser met at UBC in 1966. For the next few years they plotted various revolutions (together and separately). The details of the final one are still being worked out. Both were in on the beginning of Pulp Press. They have a long-standing appointment to meet under the clock of the Belmont on Carson's 150th birthday. Bryan Carson is a fiction writer and free-lance editor.

By D. M. Fraser:

Class Warfare

The Voice of Emma Sachs

Ignorant Armies

The Collected Works, Volume 1

IGNORANT ARMIES

D. M. FRASER

EDITED BY
BRYAN CARSON

PULP PRESS
BOOK PUBLISHERS

IGNORANT ARMIES

Published by
PULP PRESS BOOK PUBLISHERS
100-1062 Homer Street
Vancouver, B.C. Canada V6B 2W9
A Division of Arsenal Pulp Press Book Publishers Ltd.

Thanks to Linda Field and Randy Fred for their work on the D. M. Fraser archive.

The Publisher gratefully acknowledges the financial assistance of the Canada Council.

COVER: *David Lester*

PAGE DESIGN: *Mandelbrot*

PRINTING: *Hignell Printing*

TYPESETTING: *Vancouver Desktop Publishing Centre*

PRINTED AND BOUND IN CANADA

CANADIAN CATALOGUING IN PUBLICATION DATA
Fraser, D. M. (Donald Murray), 1946–1985
Ignorant armies
ISBN 0-88978-224-5
I. Carson, Bryan, 1941– II. Title.
PS8561.R295I4 1990 C813'.54 C90-091380-0
PR9199.3.F7214 1990

CONTENTS

PUBLISHER'S NOTE

The Collected Works of D. M. Fraser have been our preoccupation for some three years, during which time we released the first volume of what we had estimated to be a two-volume collection. Since then—guided by the work of Bryan Carson, who strove for many months with a mass of material intended by D. M. to be either in or out of the novel he named to the world twelve years ago as *Ignorant Armies*—we have become more intimately familiar with the archive he left behind. The result is the present volume, a text that stands magnificently on its own, a brilliant emanation of a singular spirit.

Fraser began working on *Ignorant Armies* in 1978; he was still working on it when he died in 1985. This book is the result of an intervention that Fraser himself would never have allowed: a text that bears his name, assembled by another with the connivance of still more others. If it be found wanting, let its perpetrators carry the blame; while all of the words in this text are Fraser's, they are not *all* of his words; nor are they necessarily the ones he might have chosen to publish, were he to have had the final say.

No, the final say, eerily enough, belongs to Johnny Girardi, one of the characters in *Ignorant Armies*:

> *To approach his writing through anecdote is to disservice him; but to enter through the mechanics of scholarship is to betray him. No character in the most*

explicit of his explicit stories resembles more than haphazardly any specific individual: resemblances are always imputed; incidents recalled as fact long after they had failed to occur; biography is a maze in which a reader will die of loneliness sooner than starvation. Asher held memory hostage to desire, in a low period when neither was adequate to experience. A tour of his personal history yields little insight: it is an official visit to an exploded coal-mine, or any industrial disaster, where the object of the ceremony is not to see what is there, but to be recorded as having been seen seeing it and weeping. In the only letter I received from him after his disappearance, he instructed me to finish the book he had begun, however I chose to finish it, because "the sole object of my art is continuity, that the beat go on . . ."

VENICE BY SEA

IN A PERFECT WORLD HE WOULD HAVE COME BY SEA, IN a white and graceful ship, at dawn. Walking, eager, he would then have seen through an appropriate haze, the long line of crisp sand, the row of palms along the boardwalk, the mountains still black against the light rising behind them. That was how it had always been done, this business of arrival, in a time when Nature still cherished her lovers, and they her, with a grave and proper courtesy. There would perhaps have been a slight breeze, sweet, not too disturbingly putrescent. He would have been wearing, for the occasion, a suit of fine linen. There are rules for the southern pilgrimage, and they are exacting and unchanging, though this south now includes, in its seaward prospect, petrochemical plants and gantries, hydroelectric towers, missile silos, freeways and a jetport.

The rules will be, perforce, respected by default. In the less than perfect world, Gus Asher drove south in a borrowed Volkswagen, down a highway jammed with the detritus of a summer Friday. The car was unfamiliar and untrustworthy, and he was having to give uncommon attention to the clutch.

Falsetto surfing music squeaked from the radio. Steaming into Venice, in some pale and sulphurous dawn, he would have had other accompaniment: lutes, a harpsichord, sensitively tuned mandolins. He would have remembered the correct Impressionist painting, had there been one, would have summoned to mind the essential Homeric parallel, would have quoted, to the forgiving waves, the indispensable image from a lyric of the Italian Renaissance. But on this coast, today, he will make do with boy-soprano hymns to souped-up Chevys, endless sun, the ultimate wave. Though a writer, he is not thereby necessarily a proud man. He can love, with less difficulty than one might suppose, the humility of things.

Indeed he would have been disappointed, betrayed, had this landscape been other than itself. Imagination makes stringent demands of scenery, of which the first is that it conform precisely to its own image. Thus beholding, for what we must presume to be the first time, the gas stations and motels and stucco neon of southern California, Asher allows himself, for a moment, that rapturous satisfaction which is the reward of having come, at last, to a place that is manifestly and only, always, exactly what it is. How reassuring that palm trees, glimpsed from a dusty car window in an hour of twilight and smog, so faithfully and unambiguously resemble palms. How fitting that smog itself should be, in a word, smoggy. The orderly spirit, craving a harmony in things, asks no more of the world than that it be, in the deployment of its attributes, wholly tautological. Occasionally, as now, the world obliges.

It would be false, of course, to claim that such reflections occupied more than a fraction of Asher's thought, the bulk of which was already moving, somewhat apprehensively, toward other, more problematic concerns: the availability of food and lodging, the health and well-being of the Volkswagen, the hoped-for imminence of a cool, inebriating drink. He had come a long way; he was tired; there had not been time, yet, for the habitual chill to quit altogether his shivering northern heart. There had not been time to become the tanned, confident Californian who was even now waiting, ever more restlessly, to be born in him. That this birth would eventually happen was a certainty: had he not felt, descending to the Pacific, the first sure contractions of that long overdue and difficult labour? The radio sang to him anthems of debauchery and light. The passing cars had never been so brilliant a blue, so rich a red, so innocently sunlike a yellow. What Michelangelo had fashioned the bodies that ran and danced on the beach? Asher, whose professional business it was to think such thoughts, thought them with a pleasure that, for once, owed nothing to habit. He thought them repeatedly, in a variety of sentence structures. He let them wind, as deviously as this coastal highway, through his unrepentant visions of hamburgers, french fries, chilled beer, the soft and unquestioning bed that lay prepared for him. To what he felt, now, he had neither wish nor competence to put a name. He was, he reminded himself, on holiday from his craft of naming things. But later—for there would be a later, and a later than that—it would occur to him with the thrust of a fist that at this instant, piloting his poor carriage down this alien highway, on the edge of an arrival he had never expected to accomplish, he had been happy. For almost the first verifiable time in his adult life, he had been happy.

As it happens, there are snapshots, taken with a cheap camera by strangers randomly conscripted for the job. In each of these, the background is different, but more or less what you would predict; the second requirement of scenery, directly consequential to the first, is that within a small range of variables it be predictable. (This condition, however, may not consistently be met.) But the backgrounds, though useful as evidence of certain things, are not of primary interest to us at this point. We should look rather to the foreground, which varies hardly at all from picture to picture. The foreground is Gus Asher, standing in a posture less loose than he imagined it to be, hands on hips, eyes straight ahead, gazing with a blank and blissful intensity at something just slightly past the photographer's head. These shots, if studied carefully, may tell us something of the man in whose fate we are conspiring. They would disclose infallibly the nature of his mundane occupation. If you did not already know, you would soon deduce that if Asher were not in fact a writer, he ought to have been one. There is the suggestion of myopia, that appearance of earnestness which comes less from the condition of being earnest than from the incapacity of the eyes to see, wholly, what is in front of them. There are signs of a life in which inward licentiousness and outward asceticism have made an uneasy and qualified peace. Asher, one feels, is the manner of man who would drink to excess to conceal his discomfiture at a party, and spurn, clumsily, the well-intentioned advances of a beautiful woman. He wears the assurance of the successful writer, the man of reputation, with a slight stiffness by which we perceive that he may, after all, secretly think himself a fraud. His clothes are so radically ill-fitting that we might accuse him of having deliberately fabricated this costume: perhaps to signal his principle indifference to the niceties of worldly vanity. Finally, there is his stoop, which bespeaks a waking lifetime spent in ardent and only fitfully fruitful contemplation of the typewriter.

Otherwise, in these pictures, we have a man who seems to be waiting, in a false tranquility which is merely the self-cancellation of opposites, for the approach of middle age. The hair affects the length and style of youth, and like all affectations at once shouts its impropriety. The moustache is suitably authorial, but unkempt. We have the impression, which may or may not be an accident of light, that he has forgotten to shave recently. This may or may not, like so much of his behaviour, be calculated: possibly he determined that, being on vacation, he was entitled to dispense with the routine observances of his life.

The snapshots, then, both illumine and obscure the man: we cannot know from them whether this is Asher as his accustomed world knew him, or another, ersatz Asher who existed only, and briefly, in a California which itself only existed while he lived in it.

It was strange, he thought, walking the beachfront as he did every day now, it was strange and yet not strange how illusion had penetrated into the very names of things. The boardwalk under his feet was asphalt; the Marina Hotel had not had a pleasure boat in sight, and turned its stucco shoulder to the water; the Amusement Pier offered no amusements. The local bikers called themselves the Doges. The Bridge of Sighs was an antique shop, slowly going bankrupt, the Rialto a hairdressing salon, the Piazza a pizza joint. He himself, Asher, was illusory here, seeing but not seen, knowing and unknown. Like the town's, his was an invented identity—but he was free, as no town can be, to reinvent his as often and as variously as he chose. Today, in a mood of impish protest, he'd be Asher, erudite, judicious, liberal, slightly tedious about the Important Things. Tomorrow he might have a try at being Goethe, but he'd have to read up on life, first.

Venice. In certain lights (late afternoon, early morning), if you squinted just so hard and edited your vision carefully, it looked almost as its builder must have dreamed it. The real city was drowning in the Adriatic.

The beach is whiter than other beaches; no one ever threw a butt down on it, pissed or shat on it, came on it, left the dead end of a potato chip bag to drift across it, ghostly in the weak reflection of surf. This sand was made to be shroud. There's so goddamn much of it. Miles. He'll walk it. Everything he passes is a mythology he wants, more than anything now, to believe in. Someone may or may not be walking to meet him.

The last thing he'd see would be the ocean. It was only a stretch of water, ridiculously blue and white, extending in one direction to a horizon he would never attain, and breaking in the other upon a beach impossibly wide, clean, beautiful. It was the stuff of crude snapshots to be sifted through, sadly, once the adventure was over. In a more gracious age, eloquent paintings had been painted of it, by people who, in the luxury of their innocence, had supposed themselves artists. In his childhood, a time like any other full of discontent and incontinence, he had dreamed of precisely this scene: the long line of palms, the white buildings on one side, the white sand on the other, and beyond, beyond any reasonable reckoning of that starved and bitter northern imagination, the cruelly blue and generous southern sea. Was there a figure there, on the wavy periphery of vision where beach and ocean met? In the dreams there may or may not have been: he couldn't remember.

The amateur photographer is advised, when taking pictures of the merely beautiful, always to include the human figure: the person, human, is what makes the scene signify. (They tell you this as you tour the movie studios.) So, to gratify such conventions as remain to us, we'll include the figure, the living object in our tableau. It could be, in a more pearly perfect world, this: *the lovely boy, passing on the sand; barefooted, ready for wading, his slender legs exposed above the knees.* Or it could be, inasmuch as we are now in an older and less perfect world, only the lumpy, strong, familiar shape of a loved friend, posed for a camera you hold in shaky hands and can't—quite—remember how to operate. The picture will come out blurred. Under a fouled sky, let's be grateful for soft focus. In this failing light, the figure will appear as gold; you won't be able to see the clown's face, the ordinary scars and pimples. It's getting dark, but the glow hangs on for a time. In this country the birds start to sing at midnight. Never, never, could you have dreamed it, but you did. This dream was the fizzled vision of a real estate speculator whose time came, at last, exactly as he must have wished it: *a pale and lovely Summoner seemed to smile at him, to beckon, as if to guide him toward some prodigious fulfillment* .... Never could you have known how matchlessly it would be fulfilled.

Is the figure still there? To the south, over the petroleum wastes, a common jet takes off, its trajectory implying a world vaster than this pinched heart can encompass. We are such fools. There was a moment, when you held me, when I forgave you anything: things done and yet to be done, the time, the loss, the lies. We are so wretchedly incapable of knowledge, so careless of the poor rags of knowledge we wear. If this figure, posed so handsomely at the ocean's edge, has no face, let it wear all the faces you love: in any instant, any of them will do, and it would be cheating to put a name on it.

At which moment he, our poor adventurer, is prepared to cheat. In the last moments of this movie, he will totter obscenely forward, into the last groan of the sun, toward the face that must be there. He will allow himself this.

The figure is still there. Later they'll say he was mad, that sun and disease had softened his brain, that in the possession of some incommunicable lust he made his bed in the bed from which, the historians of biology tell us, our spiny progenitors rose. Behind him the vulgar stucco imaginings of a megalomaniac entrepreneur melt into a darkening and oily sky. It is possible to hear the surf. In the bar, a band is tuning up. Beside a lifeguard station, someone is taking a piss. Choose the simplest, plainest things you can think of, and recite them to yourself. *Too soon we rise, the symbols disappear.* It was to regain that richness of your love, that I abandoned you. And for this anger there is no cure. None of this, none, is yours. Don't speak the names, don't ever utter them aloud. You have betrayed us all. *The feast, though not the love, is past and gone.* Shine on, shine on harvest moon. How dark it is. I can't see you, but I hear the stream of your piss striking the sand. They'll say I was mad, and I was, I was, oh boy was I mad. The light of thy countenance. The sound of choppers revving up at the corner.

The figure is still there. *This is the hour . . . .* No longer illumined, the shape is more distinct: it is flesh, malleable and scarred, going a bit to seed. *Here let me feast, and, feasting, still prolong . . . .* It is an unremarkable man of unforgivable beauty, standing by the water, taking a piss. No more than that. *The brief bright hour of fellowship with thee. (Here would I touch and handle things unseen.)* It is, let's say, a man he's slept with and never fucked, though the possibility must have occurred to both of them, at least once. Perhaps they were too drunk, too tired, too sick, too scared. They may have old, untranslatable jokes in common. There are times they can't stand each other's company. One owes the other a lot of money; the other remembers and forgets. One night in a sleazy bar they may or may not have picked up the barmaid, who may or may not have been a good lay. We take such risks as we presume to get away with. *The symbols disappear.* In the snapshots, in the sun, we look tanned and healthy, unlike ourselves. We smile, showing our cracked teeth. You can see us, in our incongruous sailor whites, standing in front of the holy icons. Just a little way out of the picture, something else is going on. One of us is always looking at it. *The brief bright hour.* One of us will always be looking. We are unlike ourselves. The figure is still there.

It is a man of whom you know nothing. If you have a decent stereo, the music to play on it now is Mahler's 10th: the last movement. The shape is more distinct. Tadzio died, of plague, in 19—. His last words, hitherto unrecorded, were: *Tell that dirty old man to fuck off and die.* It was a prettier speech in German. By then his beauty was corrupted past any hope of recognition; he had a beer belly and a flabby ass, and the sweet petulance of his face had hardened into the crisp flatulence of an SS subcommander. He knew all the words to Horst Wessel Lied and sang them at parties. After the war he emigrated to America and opened a real estate office in a sleepy suburb of Los Angeles where people with long hair and bad poetry congregated.

Somewhere toward the end, deserted and despised by friends, and full of a rage for which no earthly speech was or ever could be expiation, a man on the perilous crazy edge of middle age stood on a beach, in this other, newer South, hearing behind him the sublime grinding of saxophones, sounding as in his boyish northern dreams he had always known they would sound, and drums gone free; and thank god he had a flask in his pocket. *Turn the fucking volume up. Thanks.* He was standing with his back to Los Angeles, and his face to the sea. *Come not in terror.* Perhaps a hundred yards distant, a man was standing on the edge of the surf. In such a perspective, it was impossible to determine whether this apparition was facing the ocean or the land. He was no beautiful child, seductively beckoning, but the grown, stocky, unbearably valuable body (and here it must be broken) .... *And, though rebellious and perverse meanwhile* ....

Tad, baby, there ain't much time before the crunch comes down, and there's a hell of a lot to say. Will you have patience? Will you make it to the age of consent before I die of grief? I believe in nothing but the truth of art and the holiness of the heart's affections. I want to feel under my grey and palsied hand the arching of that shapely breast, ass, belly, thigh, cock and balls, calf, foot. I want to rip that sailor suit (jeez, yer mama's taste!) from off yer frame. Tad, Tad. Let me not now scream. I believe in nothing but. This. And it has taken me so long, so goddamn long, to get around to saying it. What chills me is that I might never have said it, and where would you be then, mine own? An apparition at the edge of the sea, falling forever backwards into the greasy Adriatic and not this pacific Pacific, my arms, my groin. It has taken me so long. I might never have told you. I, who died in a deck chair, years ago. Hold me. That's the way. Now put your mouth, those flawless lips, faultlessly on my warted cock. Attaboy, Tad. Try not to gag. Whatever goes down must come up. The disease I carry is older than the earth, and I carry it for you. My hands sweat, my body is a cheap garment purchased on credit, in a thrift shop I've forgotten the name of. No matter. You will redeem me if you can. At this consummation I will die, and about fucking time, too.

The figure is still there. He knows, turning back toward the world, that the choice comes now. He may stop, seize one more look, and be lost. That is the sum of what he wants. The awful thing is that he could have had it. His feet are heavy in the sand. Ahead of him is a bar full of handsome, singing strangers. Under the palms, couples move quietly, in a dance for which all his life has been rehearsal. The lights reach north toward the thrust of mountains; he looks north. *Let me not scream*. Southward there are oil refineries, an airport, military bases. To the east, a desert.

It will have been the last time, and the last thing he would see would be the ocean.

AFTER THE MURDER

THERE WAS NOTHING HE COULD DO BUT STAND there, gaping, hearing the story without hearing it. He had no training to staunch blood, bind wounds; his hands were awkward, afraid now to touch flesh they had groped for gladly enough in the old days. Blood dripped meaninglessly on the floor, on the table, on his shirt. He had to try, had to insist that the sight not sicken him. It had happened. That was all. It had happened as he ought to have known it would. His life in these last days had been a prairie highway on which, far off, it had been possible to see the approaching lights of the truck that now, as if fated, had smashed into him. There should have been time to react. There had been time. But he had not reacted. He knew: This is *it*, baby, this is the crunch. The knowledge ticked in him, itched, fizzed in his gut. Once again he would be complicit, would have to be; there was no peace; what he had thought peace had only been a false truce, a pause for rearmament. And he had not rearmed. Fool, he thought, and was surprised to hear his own voice saying it. Not you, me. What are we going to do? *We?* Why couldn't you have died in the street? I might never have had to know. Oh, oh, but I would have known. Someone would always tell me, someone, or the radio, or the papers. But I could have grieved decently then. No one would have been implicated. Now we all are. The last connection is being connected, and won't be severed again. Try to grin, say: No damage done, nothing serious, we'll fix you. Christ. *Nothing serious?* This conversation: Who saw? There were people. But it was dark. Is he dead, do you think? Yes. Think so. He will imagine this: the swiftness, the sound of it. You were looking for him, yes? Yes. And he knew? Yes. And the others knew? Yes. Well then, the goose is cooked, isn't it? Yes. Well. The choices narrow down.

GIRARDI

Whoever has known the world has found a corpse, and whoever has found a corpse, of him the world is not worthy.

—THE GOSPEL ACCORDING TO THOMAS

I HAVE, AT TIMES, BEEN BURDENED BY THINGS I HAVE seen—the bulging flesh of an obese young woman, the damaged face of an old man. I hear things which cause my mind timidity and fear—the deaths and abuses of children, the murders recited over and over again on radios and in newspapers.

I tire at my work, look out a window. The sky melts and changes with the promise of rain. The leaves turn inside out, silvered. The trucks roll by. A siren howls. I am half blind to the beauty of the world, half deaf to its miseries. And in the face of change, I am almost always mute.

I have become, I think, a sensible man. This hurts a little to admit: it seems a kind of defeat, at my age, and somehow a betrayal of Asher, who surely would never have wished me sensible.

"You'll have to finish the story yourself," he told me quite seriously, the last time we were together, "I can't do it, I don't deserve it. Only you can write the ending I want." I wasn't sure what he meant. Now, it occurs to me that I should have known, on some untutored level did know: that this least symmetrical of men nursed, all the while, an unfulfilled passion for symmetry.

But it was more than that, too. It might surprise Asher—as even I am surprised—to find me thinking about these things, writing about them, in a manner not essentially unlike his own. My assignment, I suspect, was to do precisely the opposite, as Devon would have perceived at once and done with bitter glee, and as I, though I loved Asher no less and possibly more, cannot. I wonder if Asher himself weren't aware of the ironies in this, when he pleaded with me to complete his monument: that I was really only his second choice for the job, Devon having been the first and unavailable, and that in choosing me at all he was bestowing on me an utterly inappropriate and unwanted gift.

Yes, Asher would be surprised—pained, perhaps. He had set me—it must have been deliberately—on the very road from which he himself was turning away. We would not travel it together, and to the last he would insist on mocking it, despising its destination and pitying me for seeking it. Yet it was he who had shown the way. Once he said, casually, "You realize it's my Calvinist duty to lose you?" This happened very soon after I went to live with him; until then I had never thought of myself as being his to lose. But I was. I was, and these pages—these inscriptions on the pillar—are testament to the fact.

Of course, reviewing his history, I can appreciate how my own unworthy part in it is curiously necessary. Whatever else he was, Asher was not a creature of single vision. Indeed, it may be that he saw *too much*, too many hopelessly irreconcilable possibilities and actualities, an endlessly, treacherously shifting, living jumble of configurations too complex to be told—as if the world, and his life in it, were an immense, infinitely baffling jigsaw puzzle made animate and sentient, a demented but cunning anthill of willfully elusive pieces to which he felt condemned to impart order, and could not. One of his pastimes was to invent titles for murder mysteries in the alliterative style of the old Perry Mason books: *The Case of the Maddened Midden*, *The Case of the Paralytic Paradigm*; he had hundreds of them on file. He'd quote William Carlos Williams, "No ideas but in things." But the Things Asher meant, the ones he raided for his Ideas, were alive, frighteningly articulate, and all speaking at once in a polymorphous gabble of tongues. He could be unendurable in argument: while his companions debated civilly, empirically, assuming everything to be only and exactly what it purported to be, poor Asher's multiplex antennae would be throbbing like a wireless in an Atlantic gale, receiving a Babel of signals and unable to transmit any of them intelligibly; he'd sit dangerously mute, frantically trying to compose the first perfect sentence of the several thousand he needed, minimally, for the six-hour monologue that might just conceivably define the issue at hand if everybody would please be still and listen to him. I am being unfair.

Unfair. Oh, Asher, asshole, you knew what you were doing when you charged me with this foolishness. Fuck monuments. I, buddy, if it's any satisfaction to you I won't let you down, I'll obey the orders of the world, yours, your *Finish it, write it off.*

"He wanted what was good for you," Petrov said, in a cruelly exact parody of Asher's mother saying, "I simply wanted what was good for him." Asher had loved and loathed Petrov, and it was, of all his misaffections, the most nearly mutual. They reminded each other of something they'd each laboured scrupulously to forget. "He knew what it meant," Petrov said.

We were in the bar; there would be shouting and tears and broken beer glasses; later, muttered apologies, formal, excusing nothing. We shared equal parts of a resentment not commutable by mere speech, and a love (I will call it that) which seemed to feed the memory of Asher through an ineptly assembled electrical transformer, yielding power but flaking off sparks.

PRELUDE AND THEME

JOHNNY GIRARDI CAME INTO TOWN SINGING.

Apparently we'd met, somewhere between nowhere and somewhere else, on the train, or it might have been the road, no difference, bound anyway for the end of the line; it was in the days when lines had ends, or we thought they did. Now I remember, it must have been the train we came in on, six in the morning, winter, I was expecting to meet Joan, Johnny was walking fast beside me, twice my size, guitar in one hand and my elbow in the other: *spare change?* Fifty cents, what can you perform for that, I said. Plenty, he said, as we reached the end of the line and Joan wasn't there; the line is what they string you up from if you don't perform, I said, and we're at the end of it, as close to home as we'll ever be, do you need a place to stay. Hoping the answer was no. Certain it'd be yes, as it was.

He was running from the brothers of his shotgun bride in Sicily. Gus Asher was a soft touch, then. The platform coiled and swayed, lacking Joan to hold it steady. You gripped my elbow, no steadier than I but stronger, singing but I wasn't listening, it was the one song of yours I never learned. The sky was still dark. A shadow of snow, the murky insincere snow we have on this coast in January, was smudging our eyes. I remember now, but only in part: it was a long walk down the platform, scanning for Joan but no longer supposing I'd find her; Johnny in his massive black Sally Ann greatcoat, Asher in unseasonable tweeds carried like baggage, small but unwieldy, in the crook of his arm.

Where we going?

I've got a place.

I had a place, I think; you can't imagine how hard it was, just then, to be me.

JOHNNY GIRARDI CAME INTO TOWN SINGING.

It was a long time ago as long times go, and some things are more easily remembered than others though I tell myself ease of remembering is not the object here; if I recall Johnny it's to recall that that was the winter Joan went crazy, and I too perhaps, it's to recall that we were younger than we suspected and so still dared to leave the world even as we fought it.

JOHNNY GIRARDI CAME INTO TOWN SINGING.

That's how I choose to remember it; that's how it ought to have been. I've never understood how people know where and when to begin their stories, or end them—how the imagination, that untrustworthy instrument, can identify and preserve, for some dubious eternity, the precise instant after which, as vulgar romancers say, nothing could be the same again. Of the several thousand self-indulgent, mostly illegible pages Angus Asher left behind as his down payment on futurity, a fair hundred, at least, begin with this invocation to Girardi; followed, more often than not, by an embarrassment of blank space, or by obscure misquotations from popular songs or sentimental poems of the day, or by obliquely scrawled entries in that mighty catalog of disconnected telephone numbers, uninhabited addresses, forgotten names and forgettable places the accumulation of which, across two decades of disgraceful history, seems to have been the sum of Asher's life's work.

But the phrase recurs, persists, nonetheless, in its unrevealing nakedness: Johnny Girardi came into town singing. Something must have started then, something must have finished. Among many disorderly notes perhaps pertaining to this time, I find some truncated lines from the Durrell translation of Cafavy:

When you set out on your journey to Ithaca
Ask only that the way be long . . .
Ithaca has given you your lovely journey,
Without Ithaca you would not have set out.

So that's how I'd have it remembered, in any one of the available versions; my own favourite is just a freeze-dried glimpse: of Asher and Girardi on the deck of a northbound ferry, sliding dumbly into the Great Canadian Nowhere, in the middle of the night. That story is over by now, and this is the epilogue. Meanwhile the moon is out, and full; ragged travelogical mountains brood over the water; there seems to be no sound anywhere. In this perfectly unimportant passage, ordinary sensible history is wiped out. The spirit wants to be Ulyssean, and there's no reason now to deny it such pretty hubris. Nobody's watching. The visible world, stripped for once of its cheap realism, is a backdrop Wagner would have appreciated: a free display of megalomaniacal scenery, entirely inhuman, spooked with unspeakable therefore unthinkable phantoms, unheard music—so that it is even possible to conceive, in the purple prose of the night sky, that your destination actually is Ithaca, city of disappointments, the famous excuse for all journeyings . . . . Without Ithaca you would not have set out. Remember that, if you can.

And in some such manner, long years before, Johnny Girardi came into town, singing.

JOHNNY GIRARDI CAME INTO TOWN SINGING.

He was a large man who bounced when he walked, lightly for the weight he carried, heavily for his years, and his stomach stuck out of his pants like the blunt nose of a tug. A prow, Johnny had, padded to nudge the world around without breaking it. He carried a guitar and a road-stained army surplus bag stuffed with unwashed laundry, letters from home crumpled up and never to be answered, a six-pack of empties. About the time empty graduated from adjective to noun, Johnny was born. He grew up in a small town which would also grow up, in the same period, to a bedroom suburb: a place close to Toronto but forever outside it.

Somewhere in this great disordered mass of papers, so cagily and warily assembled, are at least a dozen otherwise blank pages with one line typed on each of them: *Johnny Girardi came into town singing.* And I could never go on from there. I could never summon back what the song was; it was wordless and sinewy, a little strident, with the peculiar upbeat melancholy of a New Orleans dirge. Asher and Johnny walked down the station platform at six o'clock in the morning, side by improbable side, and Johnny was smiling at this new city, *the end of the line* he'd call it, he was smiling and smiling all over the place, loving it, bouncing against Asher, singing.

JOHNNY GIRARDI CAME TO TOWN ON AN APRIL DAY OF freak snow and bluster—the sort of weather that isn't supposed to happen here, ever. In the grey light the railway yards looked exactly like the ones he'd left behind five days earlier, when he'd hopped the first freight out of northern Ontario; but when he raised his eyes to the horizon he knew it wasn't the same place after all; so he *had* come a distance, and this was, or very nearly was, journey's end. Ragged rows of grey stucco apartment blocks, identically featureless, sprawled across impoverished hillsides; in front of him, at some incalculable remove, the meccano-set city reared sullen towers into a pewter sky. It was absolutely familiar, although he'd never been here before—familiar as a face recalled, in precise and dreadful detail, from a childhood nightmare. He had no word for vulnerable then, but that was how he felt. He had seventy-five cents, a beat-up second-hand guitar. A pack of dirty socks and

Sally Ann shirts, and an address book in which most of the names belonged to strangers. He began to walk briskly, faking purposefulness, between the lines of boxcars, aware that he'd jumped too close to the station: an amateur's mistake. Well, it was too late to worry about that now. There was no comfort in the thought. But he had always been lucky, always good at getting away with things, and there was, there had to be, a bit of comfort in that.

Johnny Girardi, thirty years old, apostle of peace and condemned survivor, came into town singing. It was a wordless song, and to his own ears now it sounded pretty tuneless, and it bore no message to the world. Johnny was cold, he was more than a little scared, and singing—even mock singing like this—was a kind of distraction. The sound of himself reminded him that he was still, probably, alive. Of course it changed nothing; it didn't warm him or make him braver; it wouldn't have disarmed the railroad cops if they'd heard it; it wouldn't fetch him the price of a beer or a Big Mac; it was just something he did, automatically, like cracking his knuckles or clawing at his beard, whenever he couldn't think of anything else to do. It was company for him, this song.

AUBADE

JOHNNY GIRARDI CAME INTO TOWN SINGING.

He was a large man who bounced when he walked, as if the size of him were filled not with mere fleshly organs but with air, or perhaps helium, as if mundane expedience alone bound him to the laws of gravity, so that at any moment he might, without warning, elect to throw off earthliness and soar—not levitate, exactly, but somehow lurch hopefully in the style of an experimental spacecraft. He swung his shoulders with the plain unconscious assurance of the born shoulder-swinger; he sang softly to himself, in a voice remarkably light for his weight, a song he'd made up that very morning, for the hell of it:

Duh-duh duh-duh duh doodle-dee-do
Duh-duh duh-duh duh doody . . .

Later there would be other words, other tunes, which I call back to mind with a crazy regret that I probably won't hear them again:

Keep your hands on the wheel, Anastasia,
Just drive that car the way you're driving me.

If you felt the way I feel, Anastasia,
We'd be riding on the bottom of the sea

. . . a song one of his fellow passengers had lately taught him. The fellow passenger was Gus Asher, specifically Professor Angus Asher though he despised the title as thoroughly as he did the job and nobody but his mother ever called him Angus, a small and entirely earthbound man who, some years after, would answer the telephone to hear Johnny Girardi say, with due astonishment, *My god, aren't you dead yet?* and who'd reply, before he could think to stop himself, *No, but I've been working on it.* The first time Johnny Girardi laid eyes on Asher he thought he was dead, because he found this anonymous, unkempt personage on the train, in the economy coach, on the floor of it if you must know, passed out in a puddle of spilled illicit beer, and Johnny had the wit to pick him up, dry him off with a railroad-issue inflatable pillow, and sit him approximately upright on his ass to be discovered dead by somebody else, with such dignity as befits a not-yet-eminent man of letters. Asher, to his shame, had the bad taste to wake up alive, a little soiled but otherwise intact, recognizably himself anyway, wondering who'd rescued him, and from what, and why, and what had he been saying, or thinking, before the dark closed down on him.

The life he was returning to was less solid than this stranger's grip. Johnny Girardi sang: about roads, crossroads, stations, lines with ends to them and lines without, love and knowledge fed down those lines like units of information into one of those vastly complex machines which Asher, ignorant of technology, had never fathomed, except that they allowed a great deal of stuff to be transmitted to somewhere from somewhere else; just as, Asher thought, deciding after all to take a cab, we in our way were transmitted here, to this.

That's absurd, said his better self, dazed from travel. I have baggage waiting, he told Johnny. Fuck it, we'll get it tomorrow, I'll pick it up. All right. It was easy, I recall when we said *To be powerless is to be free*, and I recall when we thought being free was powerlessness, the willing acceptance of it, thinking it a virtue, a sacrifice of the worst thing for the better thing, it was easy old buddy because we had nothing but ourselves to put on the fucking archetypal altar, for worse or better; I got into the cab and gave the address and the hell with my luggage, Asher said, we'll get it another time, and Johnny picked up his guitar and began another song.

He had a wonderful contraption wired to his back, a portable skyscraper fashioned out of copper tubing, army surplus canvas, leather scraps, wrapping paper and old rope, enclosing imperfectly a garden of dirty clothes some of which, intent on escape, streamed out behind him like disreputable flags of convenience. His guitar was as weathered and bruised as he was from a decade or so of misadventures, and from a string around his neck hung one of those perforated cardboard boxes old ladies use to carry their cats in, when they travel to annoy their grandchildren: once, a thousand miles ago, Johnny'd had a gerbil in it, but the gerbil in its wisdom had fucked off in Edmonton without so much as saying good-bye, and now the box sheltered only the mickey of rum he'd extracted, ever so gently, from the jacket of a sleeping drunk on the train. His jeans had been from Newfoundland to San Francisco and back, and back again, with Johnny inside them all the way; the red and gold cowboy shirt, however, was almost brand new, being one less item in the inventory of a Winnipeg department store against which Johnny, for reasons he no longer recollected exactly, bore a personal grudge—

The sea is full tonight. So, appropriately, is the moon. Sweaty and stinking after a heat wave, Asher sits at his desk by the window, grateful for the damp semblance of breeze that crawls, not blows, through the open casement. The desk itself is a chrome-and-plastic kitchenette table, of the sort still found in downwardly mobile subdivisions; the top is grainy pink, the chair Asher sits on is red leatherette. In the window of the shop across the street is a sign that says SIGNS.

That bit about the dark closing in is bullshit. People conk out, that's what happens, but the dark like Honest Nat's never closes down, it's open twenty-four hours seven days a week, earnestly aiming to please, giving refunds on demand, pointing us to the loss leaders, the dark's the friendly neighbourhood store which calls us by our names when we go in to cash bum cheques, buy defective merchandise, read the porn mags on the racks, yeah, the dark's a memory crazed and half-dead now of your arms lifting me up from the puddle of piddle I lay marinating in.

Asher woke guilty as hell (than which it's theologically impossible to be guiltier); (somehow he'd failed to die); imagining he'd heard somebody singing:

My eyes are dim, I cannot see,
I have not brought me sex with me.

That's not fair, is it? Asher freshly if bloodily shaven, as clean as a squish of bottled soap and a swipe of lukewarm water could make him, Asher in quote fresh unquote tweeds abducted with formidable difficulty from his suitcase and put on with formidable difficulty in the economy coach men's can, *Passengers will please refrain / From telling stories while the train / is late and trying hard to make up time,* what does Asher himself do but make up time, Asher looking so much like Professor Angus Asher he'd believe in himself if there were a licence for such a relationship, or a faith to include it, Asher rubbed stinkless with obscure chemicals, anointed with hygienic products, blessed with the memory of an event he'll never remember the occasion of, Asher humming variations on a theme.

My eyes are dim, I cannot see,
I don't take off my socks to pee.

Asher went in search of Johnny Girardi, whose name he didn't know, whose face he'd identify by nothing else than the grace in it.

He'll be going soon, any day now, if he goes at all: the cars and trucks in the street howling in the storm remind him of a route he started on and hasn't finished; he wonders why mobility is the desperate theme of his time. Asher is often afraid, wakes up cold and feverish at once, thinks *I should get help*, chooses against it. Don't mind my craziness, he said to Johnny Girardi years ago, without it I have nothing to give you. He regards this as a political struggle, a moral impasse; he remembers taking Johnny home to Joan, when she was embarrassed and scared as they held each other, Asher and she half-kneeling on the bed, as Johnny looked on and said, Am I in the way, is there any coffee. There wasn't. I think we found some whiskey, in the stash point under the television.

It's the last time Asher will move to Joan without fright of her, the last time she'll let him in, he thinks. There are no last times, she says, opening the clumsy door and admitting them. Her hair's a mess, her eyes are looking past them, already seeing the histories they drag, like overloaded suitcases, up the stairs behind them.

GIRARDI AND ASHER

I COULD HATE YOU," JOHNNY GIRARDI SAID. "You're the living apostle of death and destruction. That's all you fucking well know about. You and Devon and Petrov. And you'd haul me into it, too, if you could. You've already done it. Already hooked me. Go on, pull in the goddamn line."

"I have no choice then," Asher said. "That's my message to the world, is it? Tell me, and get it over with."

He was lying on his back, his feet tangled in a mess of mildewed blankets, stinking socks, cigarette butts, the rest of him naked and dirty white, very cold, sweating. The rude ground needled his skin, but he didn't mind. One can't expect The Wilderness to behave like a Holiday Inn. The sky above and behind his eyes was the perfect black in which the stars, observed for once in their proper brilliance and complexity, became at last the thing that made our word for them the popular emblem of glory, beauty, aspiration. *Stars.* How simple and stupid, Asher thought, to waste my heart on this. How necessary. He said again, shivering: "Tell me."

Somehow he'd found the road up the mountain. He hadn't been here for ten years or more—yes, certainly more than ten—and then it had been, as now, late at night, a foolish lovers' expedition into a territory unfamiliar to either. How had he remembered the way? Why had he wanted to see the place again?

"I *can't* tell you," Johnny Girardi said. He was squatting beside the furtive illegal fire they'd made, cradling the whiskey bottle in his crotch as he wheedled the stubborn coals into life. "I think this fucking fire is too guilty too burn," he said. His thighs in the smoky glow were disproportionately huge and pink, the bottle between them a parody of a cock. "Have a drink," he said, gesturing lewdly downward. "And stop worrying."

Asher tried to recall Joan: precisely how she'd raged at him as they'd laboured up the rutty little logging road, not trusting the car, or them, to survive this crazy adventure. He'd wanted to take her somewhere . . . *primitive*, that was it, somewhere utterly new to them both, solitary, dangerous. They'd just driven on and on in the dark, climbing roads they'd have to let daylight guide them back through. *Asher you asshole we have a perfectly good jesus room in the jesus motel, what are you doing*? "I want to look at the sky," he'd said. "You don't know what sky is until you've seen it out here, at night. And we've never made it on bare ground before, have we?"

Now Johnny said, "Why can't you be happy? It was your idea to come here, after all."

Like God awakening Adam, he stretched his arm toward Asher's hand, passed the bottle. Their fingers met on its neck. Asher was being pulled half-upright by Johnny's larger strength. "You fucker," Johnny whispered, hearing his own breath as loud as the futile sputtering of the fire behind him. "You didn't have to do this to me. We could of been friends."

Asher let him go, set the bottle very scrupulously, formally, on the ground between them. The whiskey was warm and faintly stale in his throat, as if Johnny's heat had infiltrated it. "Hatred is the only perfect determinism," he said. "Merely hate sufficiently and every effect will assume its knowable cause. Whatever I've done to you I did because you asked for it. Hurt is a closed system. I warned you at the start."

"Fucking philosopher."

"No. Not me. Petrov's the philosopher. He imagines that the world in itself isn't interesting or significant of anything, that the one thing that matters is the *idea* of the world. He sees it all as a kind of elegant geometrical construct, assembled and thus available to be modified by himself. Like a kid with a meccano set. I envy him the architecture of his thinking, but it's just Van der Rohe's tautology backwards: function is form. And it produces the same result. Sterility. A structure of faultless balance and integrity, that only a robot would want to live in. Whenever Petrov commits something like a human act, he feels unclean afterwards."

"Such as Joan's funeral."

"Such as that. I was too wrecked to do anything else about it. Petrov was right: the rules had to be followed, that time. The practical virtue of philosophy is that it frees you to *act*—without desire or conscience—because the act alone means nothing. It's merely gesture, to be performed or not as you see fit. But when you attach feeling to it, when you interpret it any way but abstractly, then it gets cheap and grubby. In other words, real. Therefore unimportant—that's the Petrovian paradox in its cracked nutshell. Petrov could bury Joan precisely because he didn't know her, didn't give a shit. All I could do was stand there and feel like a pig, and a murderous pig at that."

Asher stood up and walked to the cliff's edge below which, frighteningly far down, some nameless lake yawned in the moonlight. Johnny was crouching beside the fire, its reluctant flame hollowing and reshaping his broad face. Massive, primordial, in half-shadow all savage black hair and strangely delicate, almost translucent skin, a sculptor's hallucination of a man, he might have been the totem of an ancient, derelict, but still awesomely potent god, native to the place. He belongs here, Asher thought. *He belongs here.* Without realizing what I was doing, I've taken him home.

In that moment, he wanted nothing to move or change. He'd intended to say something more, but speech seemed insult; one word could smash everything to smithereens, forever, and no effort of will or love would be enough to piece it back together. He remembered another forest-god he'd once seen on mescaline, with Joan: the beautiful, beckoning, impossibly silver figure in the trees. A sightless, sharp, cruelly immobile face with

Devon's bones and planes, mouth fixed in the classic horror-movie grin of the waking dead. *Come to me*, the delusion had murmured in Devon's voice. *You know me, you always have known. Come to me and you can have me, all I am and represent, for your whole life. But I'll never let you go back.*

He and Joan are spending a few days with friends in The Country, Asher blindly presuming that nature and idleness, generously assisted by good company and good dope, will co-operate to heal them. It hasn't worked out like that. Joan is sullen, restless, alternately and equally submissive and remote. The friends have another visitor, a tall exquisite lesbian with a guitar and an Afghan hound, the latter a city dog like Asher himself, unused to woods and rocks and open water, the perversity of leashlessness. The cabin is small—a single over-crowded room with a half-loft at one end. There are obscure jealousies all around; when anyone fucks, the entire building reverberates, shakes, and the unfinished cedar walls pick up the sound and magnify it as they echo it. Love's a sonic boom, here. In the loft, Joan and Asher lie rigid and untouching on a foam pad, afraid that the weakest exhibitions of lust will send them crashing to the floor or—worse—bed beneath, embarrassed lest no audible demonstration be taken for a lack, or failure, of passion . . . .

Choose. You can come to me now, or not again . . . . That's the bargain. I am as you see me, exactly and only this, and I can give you what you hunger for more than life itself, more than mere vulgar fucking and hoping for the improbable eruption of love. I can set you free to die.

And Asher had understood then, with a certainty that froze him into consciousness, if he actually chose to go, to cross the incalculable space that divided him from the god, there truly would be no returning. *Throw down body and mind*, he'd read somewhere. No. No. *Throw it all down. Come to me.* No. While every fibre of him had wanted to scream Yes. Take me now. But he'd turned away, toward the gently lighted cabin and Joan, as the god faded and Devon's voice taunted him: *It's too late now, you won't get another chance.*

It is some time later, a few hours or days, when Devon phones, needing bread, a place to go, of course. Asher knowing what he wants.

May all our sins be forgiven.

Oh sure, Asher said, waking, just shove them up the ass and they'll be forgiven. Immediately. Grace without works. The labour of love is labour in vain. Let me sleep, Joan said. Only let me sleep. If one drug, as yet unsynthesized, if one purchase of darkness could bring me darkness, I'd be happy. I didn't think happiness had to be illegal. In the small room where Asher lay feverishly in bed, peevish at himself as he insisted on being at all humankind, at all the world—the world of simple light which kept on incarnating itself, without permission, within his miserable body and no less miserable mind—there,

Asher dreamed a sunset he'd never rise early enough to remember. Perhaps it was nothing he'd want to remember anyway: a Romantic hallucination, brainchild of his infirmity.

So his friend Petrov would dismiss it; Petrov, for whom the static bliss of the physical world was an obstacle to Progress, a counter-revolutionary thrust: the engines reversing to bring the jet to a halt before the poor lamed beast had even got off the ground. What the vision was compounded of, other people would have to show Asher. Sulphurous fumes from the mill, coke furnaces flaming through interminable winters, transmogrified by an irony of the ecology into this shabby radiance, as lovely as befouled, and for the same reason.

What do youse want from the store, Devon said. Either youse goes or I goes.

Youse go, I want nothing.

You can't believe that I ever loved him, can you? Perhaps only in the dream was it something resembling love . . . but that was enough, because it had to be. When he woke, his face had the look debauched children's faces have in old pornographic postcards. The gold hair would have made us both rich on a commodities market we lacked access to. I knew then, I knew. I tried to warn you, in the same stupid language I stole to warn myself: but it was a warning that demanded not to be heeded. What could you have done, if you'd listened? What can I do ever again, except open the door to your knock, whoever you are? For a night, the last one or the first one, for a warning, who'll care? Fast indeed might fall the eventide—but not yet: the sun imperceptibly lowering above this park, bravely continues to shine.

Jesus, Joan said, I'm sick of symbolism. The world is surely a conspiracy to afflict us with symbolism.

Asher gathers her shoulders in his hands as he would some rare material that he'll have to take to the pawnshop tomorrow. This crisis, he says, is a failure of faith, has got to be a temporary thing. Temporary, let's emphasize that. Pain comes equipped, like Cadillacs, with built-in obsolescence. Desperate measures have to be taken, or no measure will be taken at all. Long ago, Asher was pals with the Kontinental Kar Klub, even a member, sort of, though obviously the runt of someone's litter, underage and oversexed as he was. The KKK hung out in a ratshit garage, boarded up with ripped off two-by-fours. There it showed skin movies to itself, still-lifes of horses and pigs and orangutans nuzzling one another in animal embarrassment, orgies ordered from the back pages of whatever magazines weren't too overcreamed-on to be passed around the club. It was Circle Jerk City; and the lone traffic cop in town drifted in on alternate Saturdays to tell us how not to get screwed up driving drunk; and we all knew his daughter was pregnant but didn't know by whom, and we bought a Cadillac.

We bought Solly's limo, for a hundred bucks. Solly's limo was bright pink with a gold roof, which must have been why he bought it in the first place. It was a Caddy a million miles long and had backassed seats that jumped out of nowhere and tried to eat your balls when you sat on them; there was a streaky pane of glass that, at the push of a button whimsically stationed next to the ashtray, whinnied up and down between the beige leather Chauffeur Department and the dead grey suede Passenger Department. The engine was shot, but we had much fun taking it apart and staring at the pieces. There was no way, that we understood perfectly well, there was no way we'd ever put the fucker on the road.

Ladies and gentlemen, the Member of Parliament said. Boys and girls, he intoned: speak to you tonight; you stand upon the threshold; about to embark; a great adventure; you are now entering; for which your education; the future beckons; always cherish, never forget, the lofty ideals; your parents and your teachers strove; the moral fibre; this country; what it is today . . . .

Solly's Caddy sat in the Kontinental's garage, wrecked, magnificent, the fat white tires rotting into the floor boards beneath them. Mice lived there. The tiny and grey invincible creatures snuck out of their holes at midnight, it was always midnight, to chew on the underpinnings of Solly's dread and ours. Asher tried to imagine the limo in its prime, clean and shining as the New World—the only pink and gold Cadillac behemoth in a town that felt guilty dreaming about Chevrolet rag-tops. Asher tried to imagine Solly and his dowdy little wife and his fat nasal kids riding in their limousine, giving off sparks of money in the sooty twilight we always seemed to inhabit. You, Joan said, you no doubt imagined Solly cruising the waterfront, picking up waifs and fondling them on the grey suede, while you his chauffeur stayed stolidly up front chain-smoking Export plains. The Member of Parliament was sweating. Everyone within earshot was sweating. The day had been blistering, windless, heavy with the stink of rotting fish. The fish were on their way to becoming fertilizer; fields of vegetables would grow richer; the odour would linger through the summer. Now a smoky June dusk seeped into the auditorium where the Class of 63, Nostrum High, were seated—they were in fact not yet standing—on the threshold of adult life. In the perfect world the auditorium was painted pale blue and salmon; embedded randomly in the plaster were allegorical figures representing, among other virtues, Truth, Courage, and Industry. The place was packed. A full house, scrupulously dressed, assembled there to hear the legendary escape artist. On the stage, in front of a dusty red curtain, the fifty-six certified graduates arranged in rows, on folding chairs. All but the front row of chairs rested, none too securely, on ascending tiers of plywood risers, so that the boys in the back row were seated some six feet above the level of the stage, with a considerable chasm behind them. How deeply it yawned behind them!—and, if only the poor little buggers knew, in front of them. For a moment Asher must have been in perfect balance, between that-which-has-gone-before and that-which-is-to-become. Gertrude Stein, recalling Oakland, said There is no there there. This is exactly and only how I felt. You put your cock in my hands as if it didn't belong to me. It was a piece of real estate I must have inherited from a dead uncle.

Meanwhile understand, even in that imperilled bliss, that something was profoundly, permanently, fucked up. It was so easy to shed monkey tears over the words when they didn't signify anything. Solly sold furniture. His store was a mirage of unaffordable marvels, imported from Montreal to decorate the salons of store-owners' daughters. Marble coffee tables mounted on Corinthian columns. Luxurious beds with padded, tufted, red velvet headboards. Pruriently, the daughters of "Solly's customers" leaned out windows at young Asher, winking, saying, Come into my boodwar. Said the spider to the fly, and . . . and . . . crystal chandeliers outfitted with blinking lights, amber and white, dangling above our heads like your cock when I saw it for the first time—brass candelabra, Rococo loveseats on which no distant cousin of love would ever transpire.

Solly sold the illusion of elegance ghettos live by.

But how was I to know I was in a ghetto then?

I don't mind talking, Joan said, if you're up to listening. I can't edit my life for your benefit or anybody else's—shutup—I won't let myself be one of your drugstore romances; in this story, virtue's the loser from the start. Who, I said, wasted a minute thinking vice would win—they were handsome, my heroes, and rich, and they lived in the Colonies, or lonesome castles where awful secrets dropped blood in the gutters and for the price of purchase everything was guaranteed to turn out right. In the end. His dark melting eyes melted into mine, his warm sinewy strength fastened me hell-bound, his feet raw from the raw earth trod like history on my virgin face, the night, I whispered tenderly, the night is dark and I am far from home—

Never before in the history of Man, the Member of Parliament said, have the opportunities for human advancement been so—so exciting. His face was deep red and his hands, clutching a wad of notes scrawled on yellow paper, were shaking. He was the first, and if he lived long enough he'd also be the last, Conservative elected from this riding, and he felt acutely the indifference of his audience, the elders of which were only listening to him because it was their children who were lined up there on the stage. Go forth, then, he said. He scratched his armpit. Nobody was looking. Go forth courageously into the world, bearing ever on high the standards of this school, and the noble principles for which it stands.

At home—Joan, shutup, I just want to be left alone in peace—at home we lived behind the church. At sundown the brick was the grievous red of old sausage. There was a swing in the yard between—a swing, remember?—a makeshift frame, and ropes, and, a board to sit on? Between our house and the church there was a no-man's-land where children could play. I played there alone. It amazes me that I felt nothing like solitude then—though I was excused from evening service I was never far from hearing the sound of it through the wall. I swung the swing and the swing swang swung. Flanging through the air, I flew to the doleful ecstasy of Abide with Me. Fast, the choir said, falls the eventide. As summer drifted away, eventide fell faster. You didn't want me any more. You hadn't had a bath for three weeks and your mind was almost as full as your underwear. I too would fall. The darkness deepens. Abide. I imagined you. Abide was a place only I perceived the geography of; it was just remote enough to be far away, and close enough that by an act of refusal—of me? of us?—could reach it. Deep trees rooted us in their crotches. Deep sky invited me up, wonderfully alone to their pearly silence.

On the mountainside, unthinkable years later, Asher bent, picked up a rock and threw it, as fiercely as he could, into the seductive black stillness below. Whatever it struck, the impact was too far off to hear. One day I'll write about this, he thought, the language for it will sneak in and seize me as your raw beauty did, not a real live sayable truth in any of it, of course, just a prettied-up version of our beloved old lies and illusions, unless it's you the language comes home to, you, Johnny, without me, who've taught you only the vernacular of death, a not altogether useless or gratuitous lesson, all things considered, but one you'd have done quite well to skip. The language of my mind will present itself to me just once more, as love itself will, to spook me at the end of things—so that, writing of this unlikeliest of occasions, drunk and demented as I'll surely be, in some gross beer parlour on a night of full moon and empty spirit, I'll scratch them on a page and be rid of them—incongruous, isn't it? But I'll turn the job over to you. That's what I wanted you for, my son, my brother. Like

Devon with his opera, I have to thrust the story out of my too-articulate hands; I have to let the plain unedited music of the world take over. And—Johnny, I'm sorry—you are to be my instrument to that end. And there is no end, none at all. So do it, boy. Do it with my blessing. With my, call it as you see it, my, forgive me, love.

PRELUDE AND THEME

The singers arrive before the audience. They hover on the lawn in nervous clusters of young flesh, giggling and strutting, primping, perspiring, eating peanut butter sandwiches. Eleven girls, five boys, under the Delphic eye of a massive, white-haired lady, Mrs. McLachlan, who is fussing with a disobedient microphone. This is the Nostrum Young People's Glee Club, getting ready to sing at the advent of summer. The girls are wearing severe white blouses, ground-length wrap-around green skirts, grey silk sashes; they look, as they are intended to look, like their grandmothers. The boys are shapeless in loose grey flannels, white short-sleeved shirts, green bow ties, open vests of the same green. The park, too, is a composition of grey, white, and green, an Impressionist landscape in the windless haze of summer's first official evening. Mrs. McLachlan's deeply freckled shoulders rise bare and formidable out of a green Turkish frock, the very one she wore to her silver wedding party, untold years ago, when she did a belly-flop over the head table and passed out in the mayor's lap. Nostrum remembers. Nostrum cannot attend its annual Music Festival, which

Katie McLachlan directs, which is beginning now, without reviving the story.

Dignity consists in staying put where the shame is. Angus Asher, himself no stranger to shame, has lived long enough to be able to call Mrs. McLachlan Katie to her face: she who'd drilled his clumsy hands in Royal Conservatory piano exercises, she who'd popped shyly out of innocent phallic plasterboard cakes at Chamber of Commerce stags (picture the blueberry-ripple ice cream thighs, the Minervan breasts, the modest black one-piece bathing suit with filigreed straps), she who'd not hesitated to stand up proud the next day in the choir loft of Knox Presbyterian, little white paws waving fiercely as a cornered rabbit's, conducting the saved. In song: *Thou knowest Lord the see-a-crets of our heart.* Nostrum indeed forgets nothing. Hold your tongue, Angus, that's a good lad. Keep your fingers limber. One day you'll leave this town and sally forth into a world of beauty and truth, bright as the firmament. Her house was a paradise of potted ferns and brown Venetian blinds, dusty Oriental carpets, framed pictures of long-dead pianists and singers, a mouldy National Geographic in the front parlour to amuse you while you waited, trembling, for your personal recital to start.

The light was amber. The smell was of decaying African violets and, in winter, of wet rubber overshoes, wet woollen mittens, wet socks. The Jamaican housemaid let you in, seized your parka and scarf, skittered away nodding and bowing like a blackface geisha. Here was where Music lived, and Art, and Mystery, exotic romantic things brought back from obscure places known to you only through flickering slide-show travelogues, relics hoarded guiltily by generations of missionary ancestors, gathering cobwebs in the solemn green house on Temple Street. Katie McLachlan had been to Borneo, to Spain, to New York City and Vancouver; she had heard Rubenstein live, and seen Mario Lanza in The Student Prince; she'd been presented at Court; she'd declined an audience with that heathen, the Pope. She possessed that moral splendour, once thought peculiar to the spinster daughters of itinerant clergy, which allows its bearers to be as indecorous as they please, for the sake of the Higher Things. Mothlike, the Higher Things floated around her. But Katie McLachlan was no spinster. By the time Asher came into her bourne she was several times widowed, the mother of a brood of surly characters of whom the favourite, and his contemporary, was a thin, pinch-faced boy who played the bagpipes, weakly, and was always said to be queer.

This evening, everything is available to be reinvented. Memorial Park is a narrow patch of grass and ancient trees left over between the river and the rusty skeleton of Nostrum's first, bankrupt, attempt at a mall. On the western fringe a shallow row of shiplap houses survives, leaning together as if for protection, like refugees from a regime whose dissidents, instinctively fleeing, will never wholly understand that the country they're leaving has ceased to exist. In one of these houses—the spooky brown Gothic Revival, with the lopsided turret—Asher spent a portion of what he guesses must have been his childhood, though it may have been no more than an ill-timed dress rehearsal for old age. Certain unintelligible data persist in his mind: mud-brown wallpaper with salmon-pink cabbages (roses?) and wilted leaves in the pattern, peeling quietly off the walls in the middle of the night, in the dining room. *For what we are about to receive make us truly thankful O Lord Amen.* Boiled pot roast again, Reverend Mr. Butler—you never say Reverend Somebody always Reverend Mister—with spidery hands contorted like a teepee, wiggling: *This is the church and this is the steeple,* index fingers up and joined, *This is the minister*, thumbs up, *and these are the people,* remaining fingers upside down and interlocked. There was the day the King died: purple headlines in the paper. Onward Christian Soldiers on the radio. Mother in a navy blue suit Asher had never seen before, the royal coat-of-arms pinned to the lapel. "You must be good," she said. "You must be terribly good." Mrs. McLachlan let him sleep, snug as a bug in a rug, in her seal coat, in the pew. "The poor little King," she said. "Oh, my, I feel so sorry for the poor little Queen." *With the cross of Jee-zuss, going on before.*

Before what? There was a game Asher enjoyed, played in the vast haunted Upstairs, where nobody lived except to sleep. Father would lift him up to his shoulders and carry him stealthily in the dark from room to empty room, in one of which—*which one?*—Mother would be hiding, in a closet or behind a curtain, poised to spring out all of a sudden with a heart-stopping BOO; the genesis, the orthodox would say, of Asher's tricky nerves. On malevolent winter days he'd build a tent, a castle, out of sheets draped over the drying-rack in the attic. The Clothes-Horse, it was named in the family. He saw a small, shabby, weatherbeaten beast of burden staggering up the hill of the attic stairs, laden down with the deserted clothes the bums at the back door wouldn't take away. In the shelter of the clothes horse he'd retreat for hours, alone, unapproachable, whispering to himself, inventing long, intricate stories which meant something only to him. There would be few such sanctuaries again.

Asher is planted in a crotch of roots, under a huge sick elm. Behind him the river is white. Above him the leaves are the green of weathered copper. In front of him the Glee Club has been assembling itself: a tableau formed and cast in some obsolete image of loveliness, sentimentally erected on this spot and then abandoned, left to accumulate bird-droppings and acid corrosion, winter frost and spring graffiti, as though sprayed with a time-retardant to preserve the scene immaculate through all the insults of history. Down a cracked asphalt path, some distance from Angus Asher and his illusions, a pair of young persons in matching track shorts and T-shirts kiss lazily, unkiss, share a jug of applejack, roll gently together and apart as if in slow motion, in soft focus, trusting the sunburnt grass beneath them to be especially greased and oiled for their pleasure. Angus Asher feels no jealousy: he knows well how it is to make love on a bed of used condoms, on just such an evening . . . .

The street bordering the park is beginning to fill up with cars; in Nostrum, a town so compact and self-contained that anyone could pace the length of it in an hour, everybody drives everywhere. There is a mysticism of the Automobile here: the Alien God imported from afar, from the Real World beyond

Nostrum's limits but not beyond its imagination—somehow proof, as the shabby old houses and dilapidated local monuments no longer can be, that the other world lives, is even accessible, can still yield up its products for a price. To walk, as Asher has no choice but to do, is not so much eccentricity as it is heresy, sacrilege; it is to identify oneself damningly with the legions of the defeated, the capable of being defeated, the morally incompetent who've failed to reap the harvests of the Lord. Asher is quite conscious of this, sensitive as he is to the certainty that he and most of his friends—poor, haphazard, dysfunctional, displaced, *carless*—can hold no visa for heaven, and endure on earth only by the sufferance of oversight.

But now, ready for the music which will soon absorb his concentration and drain the last of his reveries, he finds a perverse comfort in the knowledge that Nostrum, whatever its affectations of well-being, is secretly as much in love with damnation as he. Child of this place, he wears its imprint more visibly than, when he goes away, he cares to admit. In his parents' house were told tales—murmured, actually, behind reticences of the dinner-table—wholly befitting the funereal Gothic Revival architecture, rumours darker and more bizarre, more thrilling to the nerve of his erotic being, than any he could compose in his own mind's tent: this seemingly sheltered little world, outwardly timeless and irradiated with Grace, was in fact a veritable sink of refined depravity. Next door Jimmie MacGregor, in a tequila fit one day, threw the Spode gravy-boat at his daughter Annie, rendering her so insensible that she promptly went and got pregnant—got herself pregnant, in the usage of the day — with the aid of Leo Holz, the Nazi sympathizer, who had kept his lights on all through the War and lived in shade forever after. Annie drowned the baby in her mother's laundry tub, left it there for the elder MacGregors to discover when they came back from Bermuda a week later; Annie caught the bus to Providence, where she took up with a minor Mafia don and from whence she returned in glory every August, unpunished and impenitent, in a three-toned Packard convertible. Her erstwhile high school sweetheart, Sgt. Jack Clooney of the RCMP, shot the MacGregors, a visiting neighbour and himself in what the newspapers described enthusiastically as a Shooting Spree; nobody died. Meanwhile the lesbian sisters, Roberta and Josie, lived and perished at the end of the block; when Josie fell or was pushed down the basement stairs and broke her skull, Roberta locked herself in the linen cupboard and starved to death. Three months later a suspicious newsboy found what was left of them. Close by what is now the Mirabel Apartments used to be Doc Watters' house; supplier of morphine to several decades of Nostrum's infirm, he eventually grew too shaky to manage a needle for himself and died in the attempt. It was Asher's own father who found Mrs. Watters' bones in Doc's medical kit and a vodka bottle of dope in the refrigerator. Asher, recollecting at random, can summon home a dozen or more such litanies of misadventure, every one of them magically interconnected with every other, related not simply by virtue of a common gruesomeness, or even a common setting, but by some generic filament they all lit up in the brain of a weird small boy with big ears and a precocious vocabulary.

Grown up, Asher shifts in his nest of roots, parked in a time-warped Nostrum still illuminated by fifties neon, still shadowed by the blackened anatomies of colliery workings disused now, still susceptible as he himself is to the blood-rushes of summer. The Glee Club is warming up, humming to Katie McLachlan's pitch-pipe, coming alive nervously, de-statued and tenderfoot on a darkening earth. Their set, flushed faces say *We're here to sing to you, dammit,* and it is of no importance that their voices will be frail, tentative, ill-matched, imperfectly trained; life itself is hardly otherwise, after all. It is of no significance that their ingenuous music will sound strange to ears grown sophisticated and half-deaf with the world's banality, their hapless sentiments sound merely silly to ears armoured against silliness. What matters here, only, is that for an escapist hour they flourish unspoiled by our cynicism, that they toot the lowly vocal instrument as best they can against the shuffle of freights in the railyards, the cries of traffic, the catcalls of pleasure boaters on the rancid river, the chatter of the audience itself. Presently Asher will be asked, *Were they really any good?*—for it is inadmissible to the intelligence of Nostrum that the homegrown product might stand comparison with the foreign—and he will say, *Yes, they were good,* meaning something utterly aloof from questions of musical aesthetics. And perforce he'll be right.

The singing begins so unconfidently, so casually, that at first Asher is hardly aware of it as a sound distinct from other sounds. It could be birds practising evensong, a distant chorus of factory whistles signalling catastrophe or a turn of shift, a yelping of tires along the County Speedway. Beside him the cultural correspondent from the Nostrum Daily Digger is already making notes with a hectic virginal earnestness, as if the meanest ceremonies of town life were the stuff of Literature. She has a child's copybook propped on the lap of her flowered print dress; her knees, drawn up almost as far as her thin, slightly whiskery chin, support a Happy Fried Chicken container on which the scribbler perches like an albino pigeon . . . . Asher, projecting furiously, feels a potent tenderness toward this naked courtship of the Word, this love unstained by intellect, uninhibited by art. Away in his remote city, lonely among his philosophers and poets, he subscribes faithfully to the Digger, not for its factual news of home but for its facsimile of home-ness: that mental country he may have renounced, may repudiate all he likes, but never can wholly vacate. Corporeally present in the very locus of his remembering, he receives everything he sees as simile. Everything is to be written down, if not by him perhaps by the Digger's muse, if not as presumably is, or was, then as it ought to be, or might have been. Everything is to be transcribed, inscribed, on newsprint or bond or lined Hilroy pages: what we weighed, what we wore, how we smelled, what forbidden Tastee Snax we extracted, furtively, from the picnic baskets of our affections, and consumed, just as furtively, with a fine display of damp paper towels . . . . Another time, Asher's friend Petrov will tell him what he himself has already understood, almost pridefully accepted: that his life, the entire universe of his invention, is nothing but analogue.

Mouths opening and shutting in approximate unison, larynxes heaving, the Glee Club shuffles to form a sort of semi-circle, a jagged tricolour crescent, with Katie McLachlan stellar in mid-curve; by squinting judiciously, Asher can hallucinate the configurations of a flag, grey, green, white, the emblem of some ideally bland, anarchic pastoral state, rippling in the breeze of human misconception. He thinks, absurdly, I must not think like this. He takes a pull of whiskey from his omnipresent flask, to silence the yammering brain. Gradually he distinguishes words clinging leechlike to the tuneless tune, a song of ostensible welcome: Hi-eye, we're the nee-oo generation. It comes across more threatening than welcoming; the illusion of innocence is mainly visual, he supposes. It's predicated on glowing peach faces, scrubbed hair, unshed baby fat, Nostrum porridge and meat loaf—nothing to do with the lived emptiness of the place, the dope flights and tavern nights, the brawls of brothers and murdering of wives, husbands, lovers, the sullen dreams of someday Getting Out, be it to Toronto or the arms of Jesus, the rescue constantly deferred, stubbornly wished for . . . . So this musical greeting, tonight, has the melancholy of a good-bye, without the conviction much less the exuberance; it occurs to Asher that these stalwart boys and lissome girls probably know, or fearfully suspect, that they are not a new generation at all, but the revivified remnant of an old one. *High, we are your children.* Not mine, he defies them, not mine. The thought leaves him unclean.

He needn't worry. The outsider, even the native outsider, is invisible in Nostrum, which sees only what it sees fit; to be here in Asher's guise is in effect not-to-be. He has his own word for the phenomenon: nontology. He grew up with it living in his marrow and it has haunted him ever since, pursued him through the labyrinths of cities and the corridors of Academe, infiltrated his rest in the beds of women and men uncursed in the imagination of Nostrum, squeezed his voice in argument and his testicles in lust, mocked all the prose which bears his name. In Memorial Park, curled between the warm knotty legs of a dying tree, he is not really there, or anywhere on earth; with his sallow skin and dun clothes wrapped into this shelter of decaying bark—something unaccountably poisoned before his birth or the birth of memory—he is at last as sublimely anonymous in his body as he has long been in his fancy. In philosophy such a compulsive rejection of identity is held to be, literally, dread-ful; in psychiatry, pathological; in certain occultisms, ecstatic. For Asher, personally, it is none of these things, but rather a near-pleasurable loosening and shucking off of the self's constraints, a release obscurely erotic in feeling. Sometimes, as now, he apprehends it as his particular, sentimental image of freedom: a casting away of ropes, a raising of the anchor. The little craft glides noiselessly from the dock in stealth of night, drifts seaward, unpiloted. But there is nothing to fear in this unseen ocean.

The Glee Club sings on, valiantly, but Asher has stopped listening.

JOAN

HOLD ME," JOAN WHISPERED TO HIM, YEARS AGO. "Any of us might drown for the hell of it." He whispered back: "I don't think I want to go down under that slimy water for the hell of it."

In another age, Asher might have said as he did say, in another age unimaginable now, We are in the hands of the Fates.

The choir, gaining confidence, is soaring full tilt into its favourite—

Oh don't de-ce-ieve me
Oh never le-eave me
How-ow could you tre-eat
A poo-or mai-den so . . . .

The choir, eleven poor maidens and five cruel lovers in flannel and baby fat, have achieved a perfect luminous faith in the principles of betrayal and forlornness, which the uninhibited soprano must always rise lyrically above, and nearly does—and this pure cry of victory for a radiant instant screams over the dilapidated elms, over the latter-day hippies up from Massachusetts for the most tedious weekend of their lives, over the still and stinking river, the steelworks, the Kirk of St. James dirty white and rotting on the green hill above Canadian Tire and McDonalds nestling into the rock—like lice, crabs, in the private places of the Almost High, ah, we were almost high, almost we saw; it might have been then Asher held Joan for what might have been the definitive contemporary usage of the vulgar verb, "to hold."

It is as if, coming as a tourist to a Holiday Inn, one were to find in one's sleek room a flowered chamberpot and hand-basin delicately set out atop the television. In a friendly dream any eccentricity is allowable; to permit this simply to be is to exercise—enjoy—the dream traveller's prerogative; here the learned responses of waking life—terror, anger, anxiety, judgement, the rule of law—do not apply.

Poor Asher lies awake in the feet of trees; out of this dream he'll never have to move. Innocent children stand in a dishevelled crescent, carolling the good news he knows already. Life is real, life is earnest. With perfect voices uncontaminated by life they sing to him, words only suitable for a world in ruin: May our sins be all forgiven. Lift up your voices. O make a joyful noise.

The light that evening was the colour of stained cardboard, a poster somebody'd spit at or pissed on.

Devon held up mominpops for nickels and dimes, played Scrabble for high stakes, won consistently, got away with everything, almost everything, when I loved him.

Around that time, Devon wrote *Ignorant Armies.* At the very moment, he told Asher later, at the very moment he'd realized the water-pistol wasn't loaded; when, in other words, everything was as spectacularly fucked up as it would ever be, then, at the very moment, Devon understood that there could be no end to the opera, that the mad lover couldn't be allowed to die (heroically, pathetically, or otherwise), that the final aria would have to be sung, in a disintegrating falsetto, while the audience was leaving the theatre. The chorus would be outside already, in the street, abusing the bodies of automobiles. Art, Devon said, was never supposed to end. There would be no point at which you could just crawl home and forget it, leave it downtown in the orchestra pit, because it would always follow you in your tracks, hooting and shouting at you, reminding yourself of itself continually, heckling you as you sobbed your pieties in bed in nightsweat . . . .

Asher leans in his tree. Nothing, Devon said, nothing thereafter would not be Art. You'd hear the mad lover's voice in your plumbing, your electricity, the disconsolate groaning of your furnace late at night, hear him in the racket of thoroughfares; howl of the back-alley misadventurers, neighbourhood kids, ladies in waiting in Safeways and laundromats, in every utterance of the 2 a.m. wrap-up news. This would be the last available purchase of immortality. Your hair like fireflies in straw would burn in bars I never drank in; your eyes would put the smoulder out. This would be you, Joan, whom I cast out. Every noise everywhere would be an extension of life, miraculous as if believed in. I liked to think it was the life of Devon's art.

"Opera," he said, "is the plural of work. We don't only do it once. Whatever we see, whatever we hear, whatever moves us, whatever pushes on and away, it is the plural of what we once conceived, once loved, once trashed, once remembered, and now must abide with the unending knowledge of."

Asher listened, I listened. It was quite possible to accept it: that Devon's lover, having once been given leave to start his song, could go on caterwauling through the rest of history, the rest of our time. The dying song, being endless, would allow death no admission at any price, no opportunity to steal from us those illusions, those passions, which give us the weakness to know ourselves.

It was hardly surprising, then, that Devon's opera was seldom performed.

It *was* recorded, once, and Asher, himself straitened in his sex, was present for the ceremony. Devon was famous by then; we hadn't met or spoken for a long time. His pardon was official: things had reached the point at which the blessing of the government was no longer important to us, we were so unimportant to each other that we probably passed on the street a thousand times, without a glimmer of recognition. Eli, counter-tenor, was back, after a decade of absence, to the wretched little town he'd grown up in and fled from—*fairy, fairy, why don't you talk like a man, fucken little cocksucker.* Eli's brother Jeff was dead, who'd stayed behind to inherit the GM dealership, the family stucco, the local pity for the faggot brother who'd run away to London to study, what was it, music. Eli, who, according to legend, made his operatic debut in *Ignorant Armies* on the very night that you, Devon, threw him calmly out of bed and house and heart . . .

It was called the pinnacle of their career.

The day after Jeff's funeral, Eli gave his concert in the town hall. Devon, looking dangerously thin and foolish, sat at the grand piano Jeff, in a mood of peculiar defiance, had donated—contributed?—to the citizens of Nostrum, Nova Scotia, in his brother's name; the centrepiece of the show was to be the Mad Scene from *Ignorant Armies.*

"I wonder what they thought of it," Joan said. "They must have hated it, all that screaming and yelling about the ruin of the world. Their world so fixed of old and founded strong, or something. Therefore the heart will break in twain, or something. We die, or something. What's wrong with thinking positive for a change?"

"Yes, I'm sure they hated it," I said.

In Nostrum, the music, Devon's and mine, lurched through the squeakers of a sound system gone haywire; Eli's voice as though in memory filled a hall ten years and a Civic Improvement improved; I was telling Joan what little I could summon back of that, how I was the asshole who actually wrote the actual words, drunk one night when our love was leaving us; the words were meant to be an unspeakable message to you, Devon, but you misunderstood and thought they were a poem—and that's how, as if by accident, they became the text of the most notoriously unperformable opera in the world.

So I was reminding Joan about that night in the Nostrum Town Hall—*Was I there?* You bet your delusions of grandeur you were. And your delusions of reference, too. Grimed sick-room-mildewed walls. A full house, scrupulously well-dressed, there to hear the legendary home-town escape artist.

The singing was less than perfect, which was how you surely wanted it. You wanted it to sound like the scraping of ten-dollar shoes on the mud around Jeff's grave, yesterday, like the credit-hungry murmur of Chevy buyers in the agency, like our talk, croaked as I croak now to Joan; you wanted the microphone in front of you to be twisted and tilted, inadequate as my love, or yours, while the paid-for technicians scrounged for tail in the beer parlour down the block. *Swift to its close ebbs out life's little day*—what with Jeff so recently dead he can almost be an excuse for this memorial, Eli sour in the gut and head, old Rotary buddies farting in the audience, yourself now thick and squat, drooling above the keyboard, the only fucking Steinway in Nostrum, reinventing the notes you were too sad to sight-read from the score, thinking, *This is a recording, Asher, sometimes he's in bed with a beautiful stranger, will hear us, lying at last parted from her, his—what was the word he used?—incomparable thighs, cunt, whiskey breath, owe him so fucken indifferent to her resounding lack of load of him—this will touch him then.*

So it did, sweetheart, so it did.

Ah, Joan, yes, didn't it.

We heaved in the mattress, that ratty oblong of foam you had the kindness to let us share, while Eli's voice, in its decline, howled to us sentences I'd forgotten authoring. The burghers of Nostrum coughed and belched, applied polite hands to impolite itches, contempted, in the background. *Change and decay in all around I see . . . .* Summer light lay over us as if to smother us as it no doubt did for you, always Nostrum, but Joan is kindly, used to as used by my failures—*I do not know—what is this, some kind of epistemological question?*—oh fuck you we lie and listen as you'd wish us to, if you knew. I myself, Devon, do not know—

DEVON

THAT WOULD BE YOU, THEN?

That would be me, the telephone says.

Trouble?

How did you guess?

Dreamer, I didn't have to guess, tried to warn you, remember?

Yeah?

Yeah. In the bar, remember? We were fighting, or so it seemed. What had we to fight about? It couldn't have been politics; that came later; that was after hope and desire walked away into your personal sunset; the slaughter by then had achieved such magnitude that even you noticed it, and the notes I was leaving beside our bed had achieved such craziness that even you shivered when you read them; you were getting cold feet, clammy fingers on the water-pistol. In the evenings, when the air was fuzzy, you put your sounds under my typewritten tongue. We fought a lot. About money, food, liquor, rent, who'd cheated at cards; about the little girls you conscripted off the street and brought home, terrified; we fought because I sent them away before you could plant your seed of terror in them—before I could. You thought me jealous. I was discovering things that never made it to the scraps of recycled newsprint I abandoned for you. *Ignorant Armies* was a gleam in your eyes that glistened as you turned, wetly, to Asher who lay scared beside you in those days, who wondered what the flying fuck you were seeing, or hearing, in those nights when you were dreaming the aria that wouldn't end, that would preserve and prolong all the noises of the world, forever, and it was I who presumed you'd chosen me to write the libretto . . .

But death and terror were all around us. People no stupider than us were joining cults. So it was relief of a kind to fight with me, then to stomp off, huffy in the pride you didn't suppose I'd understand, leaving me behind to water my beer, I was embarrassed, it was so damn obvious. Asher never liked a scene. You in your shapely musical head were already composing a scene, the final one for the sake of which I'd go home that time and frantically scrawl some more bullshit, but I didn't know that immediately, I comprehended nothing, I sat down at the table and watched you disappear. Keep it private, keep it secret.

As if we ever had been a secret: the crowd at the next table knew all about us. They were dealers like you'd been, most of them, small-timers—what's the newspaper term? Lower Echelon. And spooked, it was a time to be spooked in. Any of us all might be the next to go. Where?

I'm getting out, Devon said. Easy enough to go east, change my name. It's not as though it hasn't been done before.

Asher understood that even he could do it, too. Identities were flexible because they had to be if you had any intention of surviving. Dangerous to fix too knowably your name or character or locale; the more masks you had available the less chance you'd get caught behind any one of them. In those days every act of moving in presupposed the inevitability of getting out. We lived from backpacks and shopping bags in expensive leased apartments we were always ready to break the leases of at a moment's lack of notice or failure at disclosure. We bought nothing we could not more easily steal, since stolen goods can be left behind with less grief of dispossession, and while we were none of us dispossessed in the historical sense, we were utterly convinced that we were just about to be.

But there's no such place as Out, is there? Had there been, perhaps Asher would've gone with you, after all. He was, god have mercy on him, growing attached: not as yet to anything material, but to an idea of stability that appeared more attractive the less probable it seemed that he would ever be privileged to live it. What he wanted was continuity—the trust that what was present for him this morning would be present tonight, that what he knew today would still qualify as knowledge tomorrow. That yearning, which he would have been ashamed to speak of to the likes of Devon (who had done without it so splendidly for so long), precluded any simple business of escape.

When you left, the bar was suddenly quiet. I'd never heard it so quiet there. Someone eyed me very intently, then came over. Lank dun hair tucked into the collar of a wormy lumber jacket, eyes better suited to closing deals than making contact. *Can I?* Oh sure. *Your buddy there, who split, a good friend?* Sort of. It seemed prudent to be stingy with the truth. It was. *Listen, it's the crunch, shit's gettin' ready to fly.* I contemplated the prospect; in the abstract it was meaningless, it refused to connect with me, with Devon, with our life. Or, if it connected, it was as an hallucination out of some imaginary past—a story. *I mean it. You tell the little snot, if you think you love him so fucking much. I seen you crying when he snuck out. There's assholes around that know all about him, who he is, where he lives, the whole fucking pile of it, you better tell him.* Thanks, I said. I was afraid to ask the necessary question. Thanks, I'll tell him, I said, wondering whether I had the nerve.

When you came back, repentant and grieving, more annoyed at yourself than, for once, at me, I told you. Things have come to the crunch, I said. They're on to you, I said. And you said: Don't bother me with that crap now, please. It's not important any more, you said. You looked across to where the lank-haired stranger was sitting; and you lifted your beer glass in a gesture that appeared to be either an ironic toast to me, or a curse on him.

The fuck it doesn't matter. You'll need bread, a place to go. You don't expect to come home with me, do you?

Then we'll take a room upstairs. This is a hotel, isn't it?

Here? OK.

Asher remembers little of that night thereafter. They'd got the room from a surly clerk who'd at once assumed that they wanted a double bed and charged them extra for the discomfort of it. Five flights up in a labyrinth of linoleum-floored corridors lit by naked bulbs: chicken scratchings on the walls conveyed the essential intermural messages of the place. 507 gives head. 512 is a ripoff. Beware rats in 521. We had 522. Devon wedged the tin bureau under the doorknob, then unwedged it again because we'd forgotten to stock up on cigarettes and I had to go back down to the lobby to get some. There was no toilet that flushed on the entire floor, and when we pissed in the sink, it declined to drain. The window wouldn't open—this on the worst night of an August heat wave. There was a southern European odour of typhoid, cholera, and obscure venereal infection, a distinctly Canadian odour of stale Lysol. One was not more comforting than the other. The cries and groans of fucking couples in nearby rooms did not encourage us to emulate them: never in Asher's limited experience had the thought of sexual congress been more unpleasant. There was nothing to do but lie there inert, waiting for the door and its flimsy reinforcement to be kicked in and both of us to be submitted to whatever species of crude justice we believed ourselves to be hiding from.

Devon saw no humour in it. Neither did Asher, though he scanned his repertory of third-rate jokes in the hope of finding one that would bring to Devon's unaccountable boyish face the reluctant grin which had first moved him when they met.

Not remembering, beyond the details of what might as well have been any of a few hundred sordid rooms in which his darker nights have been dreamed, Asher will reconstruct shamelessly this night with Devon. He will improve it for you. He will tell you, Joan, that notwithstanding the heat and the stench and their negative capability of lust, he and Devon removed their clothes and fell into the nest of rotten ticking that was to be their bed. He will swear that somehow, bored with listening for sinister footsteps in the hallway, and yet more profoundly bored with each other, they resurrected a semblance of love. It may have been that there was nothing else sufficiently distracting to pass the time. It may even have been that something approximate to love was actually there, between these untrue minds, needing only some such grotesque circumstance to confirm it, to marry them. But Asher does not have to concoct the memory of waking the next morning tangled up with Devon, or the sly pleasure he took when, dripping sweat, he looked down on the still unconscious flesh of his sometime lover, whose lips were curved in the infinitely forgivable rictus of the satisfied. So it must have been, in spite of itself, a good night. Asher takes his poor comprehension of the Good from such awakenings: from the certainty he has carried wherever he's gone since fleeing the bleak theologies of his childhood: that goodness is only significant when it's accidental and involuntary, shared helplessly under duress.

THE MAD SCENE

IN THE MAD SCENE, MUCH OF THE RECITATIVE IS CONDUCTED on the telephone, like this, Joan, in an apartment that might be Asher's. According to the libretto it's a Sunday afternoon toward the end of August, but Asher having failed at the measure of days it could be whatever you like. You and I both switched events in time to suit our sense of rhythm; making it Sunday nearly allows us to get off a few smart metaphors, which I'm sure you'll get around to if I don't. Truth is, I don't any longer know precisely when it was.

I'll be over, Devon said, and that was not a statement with which it was permissible to take exception.

And why not? Nobody'll think of looking for Devon here, in our innocuous household: this dull crew growing daily more settled, more tame, jes' spendin' your average quiet Sabbath at home. Ordinary talk in the kitchen: ambiguities of orgasm, abortion, divorce. That Time of the Month. Petrov reads The Economist in the bathroom. Julie reclines silent in her catatonic corner, stringing ropes for yet another lampshade. Her kids are trying to romp in the back yard, among the shards of scrap metal left behind by a dead sculptor whose vision of the ineffable rusted away faster than he could sculpt it. Waiting for Devon, I think: be grateful for the children; they're the best cover. Camouflage for our lives. Childish innocence turneth away hassle.

How safe we seem. No enemy would dream of muscling in on this delicate domesticity, no power be vain enough to breach this peace. Asher's in his study, noodling notes for what will become, through no deliberate agency of his own, Devon's opera. As for the criminal class (of which he's now an accredited acolyte), it appears to be a fiction of something large and ungovernable called the Media, believed in by nice people whose standards of belief have fallen so low in recent times; the criminal class is obviously elsewhere than here, committing the criminal offences it's famous for being good at—skulking: no one skulks where we are, Asher has never, for example, known a real live criminal who made up an effective story about itself, least of all a true one; as we know, the celebrated exceptions have always been pardoned. Devon himself wasn't so much pardoned as neglected. By the time the world finally shut up and started listening to his music, it would have been awkward for any self-declared democracy to prosecute the composer of it. We were gambling on that.

So Devon came to stay with us for a while. Us—meaning whoever happened to be cohabiting with Asher and his ghosts. Labouring to reconstruct my folly, I want to smash the radio that, years after the event, summons it back. I want to throttle the mid-Atlantic accented commentator: This music reflects (etc). I lean at an acute angle over the mattress's edge, away from Joan, exploring for the ashtray I've lost in the trackless, what's the word, wastes of floor. Is Joan beautiful now? Among my ruins I find these clues: tawny hair, amber eyes, breasts like . . . something aggressively erased, inadmissible. It was her strength to be afraid of beauty. I can't make anyone hear what I hear, Devon said; nor I, I said, make anyone see what I'm not sure I have the power to see. We're everyone's secret. It's only to implicate myself I huddle above these words, at some cozy remove from the thick of the action. You'd say it's to save myself I have to contort and confound my tales, make them crazy as the dead man's dreams they ask to survive me.

Devon claimed to love me when I raved like this; but I can't expect to have it both ways.

When the crunch comes again, in whichever shape, what I'll fetch back to mind is chiefly the amazing weight of you on me, your head like concrete on my belly, your gaze open-eyed and brilliant in the half-light. Brilliant with love? I doubt it. But never mind. Only in dreams was it ever love. Such fancies were far too frail to endure the nights we held them through, while I snored dumbly in the crook of your corrupt flesh you were already orchestrating the song that would abide as long as sound sounded.

I digress.

The glamour of this darkness, the mad lover sings. At twilight, daring again to listen to it because I'm alone and there's no one to watch it meaning something to me—it's inconceivable that I ever had anything to do with this, so beautiful it still lights a decade of forgetfulness—oh fuck, I know what it is, the poison of that darkness. I haven't forgotten altogether, my bad habits persist though I pretend to break them. Our dead-end enterprise, Devon, is no more than a feeble compensation for a lifetime of inaction, of spying blind into other folks' lives, ourselves having none of interest to live. I'd like to ask you, Sir, where you derive your material? That was the network interviewer talking, in granny glasses and a paisley shirt, at Eli's concert. We were almost grown up by then. Hell, Asher said with false modesty, I dunno. It arrives, the material. As you did, once.

I'll digress again.

You have a Romantic attraction, my friend Petrov will say, to vicarious danger. You love the underworld so deeply because you expect to go to hell. I can't argue with him. In earliest religious childhood I grasped the point of it all: Hell was the very thick of the action. Hell was where you and your buddies would be united again on that inglorious shore. Otherwise why would they have expended so much time, so many warm and sonorous words talking about it?

(Well, you see, I just find my material where it lies. Where it lies down, panting, in the middle of the night. And with whom. Here, for instance. Had I not known Asher, there'd have been no mad scene, had I not traded Asher for Eli there'd have been no one to sing it, had you not hid me when I needed hiding I'd have wound up in jail, or dead, or both. You might say we were all in over our head. Heads.)

WEIRD CHILD

YES PETROV, I WAS A WEIRD CHILD. THE OTHER LITTLE ones round about say peaches-and-cream Holy Heaven radiant in the twilit sky, Seductive as can be Our Father Himself leaning fatherly down out of the eternally setting sun, sweetly sighing Come unto Me. I came unto Him. But I saw nothing up there but smog and a prospect of smutty temptations to which I'd happily have succumbed. (Manuscript note to Joan: "succumbed," a favourite word of Devon's about which you enquired the meaning, means literally to lie underneath. Enough said.) Possessing no aptitude for devotion, I swung on my back yard swing, solitary, on Sunday evenings like this: reciting precociously erotic fables about lovely mad women who lived in shanties on forbidden ground and gently waylaid, tenderly fondled, little Asher the intrepid. The dreaded Bad Man in the Woods did much the same, and no worse. Tramps. Scarlet ladies. Anything that moved that had a body to give was generous to Asher in the privacy of worship. The world was a maze of fascinating streets, song-blessed streets, every last mothering one of them leading crookedly to hell. I could hardly wait to be on the milky way. I swung as high as the rope would bear me, wonderfully alone and unquestioned in the

Sunday sky, joying in the hard slab beneath my bum, the strain of the rope, the weightlessness, the impure air whooshing past my greedy mouth, the beautiful risk of falling off . . . .

JOAN HONEY

EVEN SO, JOAN HONEY, BELIEVE ME, I'M NOT excusing anything. Or I don't think I am. I did what Devon asked because it was Devon doing the asking. I said, They won't look here for you. Relax, there's even a church down the block, Sanctuary. I don't think they're allowed to bust you inside a church. Consider it, if you will, as I'd have you consider me, a sanctuary extended endlessly outward to enclose this house, these anxious lives within: an only slightly better protection than any you'd pay for. I'll hold you while I can. I'll put the music on loud, so we won't hear ourselves fight. I'll bribe Petrov with whiskey to run interference at the door; what force of Right would presume to blunder past his Left? I said these things, Joan, with wholly unowned confidence, thinking of the dogs and whistles and sirens and god didn't know what else already primed to shatter our ease, that tranquil afternoon—the noises of the world that would follow Devon's mad lover into the streets of his audience, for ever and ever, as indeed they were to follow you, myself, all of our chorus. Later, if we're in a mind to hear something different, we can eavesdrop on the choir galloping through one more unseemly fast take of Abide With Me.

Thou on my head in early youth didst smile;
And, though rebellious and perverse meanwhile
Thou hast not left me, oft as I left Thee;
On to the close, Oh Lord, abide with me.

This being a siege, we'd better recall something suitable for the siege-mentality. Eli in Nostrum hovers backstage in a curtained hole, sweating. This is the premiere of *Ignorant Armies.* His brother is dead. It seems to Eli monstrously irrational of the gods to have bumped off poor Jeff, who did everything according to the rules, while he himself remains monotonously alive. When had he first understood that if the world wasn't Jeff's for the taking, it ought to be? Yesterday at the grave Jeff had been returned to his element efficiently, as—let's admit it—naturally as he resided above it. The hearse, Eli'd noted with dreadful satisfaction, was a Ford product; no one in Nostrum would have been surprised if Jeff, whose Chevy-Olds-Cadillac dealership had just gone into receivership, had risen up from his coffin in outrage at such a slight. You can't arrange everything to perfection. Tonight is the memorial service, in honour of which Eli has chosen to perform Devon's opera for the first time anywhere. Tomorrow his sister Kathy, long since nicknamed Sweetiegirl, graduates from Nostrum High. We are all present for this orgy of remembrance and futurity. The June air is rich, the stubborn light a smoky yellow, the tone of Devon's hair. Devon and I are also backstage, also sweating, sitting on a sawhorse drinking rye from styrofoam cups. Eli knows the written text of his aria by heart, but there's an unavoidable screw-up built into the libretto, which is this: should he forget the words, he is entitled to improvise at will, but should he actually remember them, he's then required to forget or abandon them at an unspecified point of his own or the accompanist's choosing. It does not simplify things that Devon, with whom he has recently been on less than civil terms, had volunteered to play the accompaniment, and Devon's habitual style of pianism is radically at odds with his style of composition. Eli finds all this intellectually befogging, and Devon getting looped on Alberta Export behind the curtain is no help whatsoever. Having produced *Ignorant Armies*, Devon feels no obligation to interpret it.

Devon feels no obligation, period, said Petrov later. It occurred to me that if I ever had to quote this man in a god forbid "literary" context, the brave finality of his utterances would be compromised by their own form. His periods would, by law, be followed by commas.

Nonetheless, the performance begins. *I myself,* Eli begins to sing, *I myself do not know . . . .*

At the outset, Asher had wished to learn everything learnable about Devon and his elm-shady past, not suspecting or perhaps not caring that the past was far from finished, or that its persistence might have certain more or less predictable consequences for the two of them. Or that the glamour of darkness might continue to mass a nest of very living real things kissing and sucking and growing steadily stronger while they awaited their escape. To Asher, sold on his own secret symbology, there was an imaginary chasm, across which mere consequence couldn't pass, between Devon and himself and Devon in the world. Scary tales told in bed had no more substance than the horror novels Asher had earlier read there in his insomniac solitude. Apparently Devon had knifed somebody: whether intentionally or not was unclear and, by Asher, a question unpursued. Somebody in any event had fallen at Devon's rotten feet in the Farragut Hotel, in a room not unlike that one where Asher at a low point in life had stashed himself and his companion; and this somebody had not been a likable or an honourable man, nor had he likable or honourable friends, and though it was Devon's luck despite his full catalogue of filthy habits to have motherlovable looks and an actor's fluency, so that he contrived effortlessly to stroll out of the room and down the stairs and through the greasy lobby and into the beer parlour without bestirring the least curiosity in anyone who might have observed him, though for several hours afterwards he bought beer for, and drank and joked and traded ribaldries of the most banal sort with, somebody's unlikable and dishonourable friends, who could scarcely have been unaware of or indifferent to the bad blood now spilt upstairs by Devon's hand or more precisely by his knife, and though in some quarters of the city this murder (or it may have been manslaughter) could have been regarded with not inconceivably justified gratitude and not inconceivably merited forgiveness, so that Devon could have told and embellished the story at his pleasure, all of it having taken place so swiftly that he could go on sleeping guilelessly in Asher's bed after telling it, despite the likelihood—no, the certainty—that revenge could be and according to Asher's warning even then was being entertained, Devon himself was still breathing easy and undamaged, fearless, only sometimes fearful, and the shadow of probability was for Asher a bedtime frisson, as in the enactment of a Guignol in which painted puppets die and revive in time for curtain calls before an audience already restless and thinking of other concerns: dinner, blow jobs, aesthetic questions, the miserable weather outside the warmly upholstered theatre. The Exit sign means what it says.

Asher had met Devon in the club where Joan slung drinks to supplement her arts grant, where Devon was playing a not very persuasive rinky-dink piano for tips and contacts, where Asher had trailed one of a succession of fleshly illusions at the near end of a too-long night of beer and bad-mouthing. Conversation in such circumstances can be costly, as Asher was surely wise enough by then to appreciate. But wisdom has a way of being undependable at three o'clock in the morning, and perhaps there was in him a gambler's tired desperation which made him for once, dishevelled appearance notwithstanding, unreasonably attractive to Devon. Or the Tiffany light was deceptive, the scene contagiously charged. Or Devon too was drunk. Little was said, and in the months to come there would be queries which Asher knew better than to make. But there was a recognition that moved between them in small, unspeakable signals of need: and it had been a long time since Asher had seen in another face, or in the reaching out of other hands than his own, the admission of anything like need. This astonished him. Still later, when it seemed he knew more about Devon than his wobbly peace of mind could endure, when in truth the crunch had come and it required all their combined energy to live as if it hadn't, by that lateness it was incontrovertibly too late to wonder aloud just what in heaven's name had brought

Devon first to Asher's table and subsequently, almost unbidden, to his appalled but amenable arms.

IN THE AFTERMATH

THAT DEVON WAS A COMPOSER OF SOME SMALL repute and somewhat larger gifts seemed appealingly incongruous—Devon with his dope and his cheap stick-ups and his omni-horniness and the debris-strewn two-room cold-water flat in which, that first night, and many others to follow, they discovered what they could and couldn't do for, with, and to each other. To be fair, it soon enough became evident that what they could do was, though far from unappetizing within its limits, insufficient. What Asher told himself, through the hours of aftermath and sleeplessness, was that Devon demanded too much and returned too little, that he was faithless, that he was mendacious in his loves as in much else in his life, that he plainly wasn't worth, had never been worth, the bruises he routinely administered, that however talented he was nevertheless shallow of heart, ungenerous of mind, cloudy of will, that he was even then beginning to corrode, that his celebrated expertise as a lover was after all negligible, that love is as love doth and Devon's love was peculiarly dothless if one were to assess it objectively, that the hard berries of the matter were that Devon had been a great big mistake from the start and only Asher's unreasoning lust in tandem with some flatulently and fraudulently perverse metaphysical distemper had darkened him, Asher, to the obvious.

Asher in the aftermath told himself these things with a supreme confidence that survived, at a modest estimate, twenty-four hours. He appropriated his vocabulary of dismissal from the commonplaces of romance, he remembered and savoured the whole drear lexicon of hurt, he lay determinedly awake composing insults, abuses, every available incidence of betrayal, he sang litanies of repudiation, he gloated fiercely in this proof, so long and so foolishly and so woundingly denied, that love between men is unnatural and transient and moreover impossible and moreover destructive and moreover over, at least for the present, in other words everything the Philistines always said it was, and hadn't he also always known it, really, in his secret of secrets, and now thank god or the devil he could go back to Joan and cry her mercy and be given it and be received once again into her mercy not to mention her heretofore too casually and too wrongly disregarded cunt, her hospitable cunt for are not cunts ever hospitable or meant to be and all would be well and he'd be home safe and all would be very well and the shame and the nervousness the hiding the lies and bullshit the precious pretence of defiance the failure of defiance the failures of cock failures of pride dignity sanity sensibility thought hope heart would be over forever and ever a-fucking-men and that would be that would be that and the beast that had burdened him strangled mangled him ragged him ripped his very guts open and eaten him his heart liver kidneys bladder balls that had seized him by the short hairs in a grip of firesulphuricacid a lather of shit and vomit gangrene and pus would be over over permanently finally absolutely over and done with and gone and consigned for all time hereafter to the hell whence Devon had crawled and back to which he could fucking well crawl now and Joan would bear all things believe all things and Asher so hopeless in love would no more be hopeless in love and Asher would bear and believe all things too and Asher so inept so tightass in love would learn love at last.

All of which, perforce, came slightly to pass.

Asher, Joan would say after Devon was gone, why do you always have to turn love into an education? Why not simply enjoy it? Nobody really wants to be your teacher. He knew it was true, of course, that was what he continually went after, the Learning Experience he leeched from friends and lovers time after time, though it must have occurred to him—did occur to him—that in point of painful fact he wasn't learning very much of intrinsic value or extrinsic use, it was a wickedly expensive and singularly unprofitable education he was buying (or stealing), and what he had to show for it was merely a grab-bag assortment of eccentric skills which became obsolete immediately upon being applied. There is, for example, no job market for sympathetic madness. Asher might have contemplated setting himself up as the expert criminal abettor he was, but it's not a talent one especially cares to advertise. Or: what audience would pay to watch mental self-laceration, even in these days of kinky entertainments. So Asher leaped merrily into Devon's suspiciously ready embrace believing against all the lessons of his life that the experience would be Good for Him, would make a better man of him, would lead him by the trusting hand through whatever hells to that knowledge the Lower Depths alone can yield (as he told himself). And Devon thought it was only sex he wanted.

Happiness for a time, then, not untinged with a little pleasurable terror. Locked doors, drawn drapes, held breath when feet came up the stairs, when knocks sounded, or sirens went by in the street. All much more theatrical than strictly necessary, sure, part of a game of menace to spice their otherwise commonplace routines, but it was a harmless enough fantasy, like the underworld movies they liked to watch together identifying thrillingly with shady characters quite unlike themselves in reality. Happiness for Asher who loved not fleshly Devon but the possible idea of Devon. Asher reading lurid tales in newspapers thinking childishly I know something you don't know haha whenever he recognized a name or incident from Devon's ample repertory, gleefully escorting bumpkinesque out-of-town friends to low bars and clubs, savouring their shock, or conversely introducing Devon to his own more or less sophisticated milieu, which disappointingly received him, as he did it, with bemused equanimity, not an eyebrow being lifted even on the occasion when, going at it steamily during an otherwise tedious party, they were intruded on unawares by the host's mother. How wonderful, how freeing it was for Asher, who let's remember had grown up amidst the rigors and repressions of less enlightened times and places, who'd never so much as seen a verifiable drag queen for instance until that very year, who'd never before slept with anybody who kept a knife under the pillow with the taken-for-granted expectation of one day having to use it, whose knowledge of evil had always been picked judiciously out of fictions and fantasies, who was so keen to know everything that he badgered Devon for weeks to initiate him into the art of the hypodermic though Devon himself had long since kicked, and as it turned out Asher's hands were too unsteady with excitement to hold the needle so that Devon had to shoot him up and *absolutely nothing happened* . . . . Poor Asher, failure in all things, but such minor humiliations didn't greatly impair his happiness, at least he'd tried, a man on his vacation ought always to try something new, however unsuccessfully.

Vacation it was, though Asher wouldn't have called it that. When he let himself picture a life with Devon, which at moments seemed an attainable prospect, there were any number of things he scrupulously neglected to consider. He was aware, yes, that to know in bed is to know in part, but what he didn't know about Devon was precisely what he needed to, and couldn't, know. Sentimental Asher liked walks on the beach, at twilight, that extraordinary light that filled and burned him; Devon hated Nature as if the poor bitch had done him wrong. She had, but was it fair to take it out on the beaches Asher loved, the absurd postcardly vistas he still permitted, against his saner judgement, to touch him? Asher and Devon would never stroll complacently on beaches, never squander peaceful hours in museums, never . . . . Asher'd had glimpses, little more than that, of what existed to be savoured and cherished in the world, *qualities of light* was what he'd say, things altogether alien to what Devon was and represented, you could not if you tried envision Asher and Devon at Tintern Abbey or in St. Mark's Square unless they were panhandling or waiting for a score, they'd never climb Mount Athos together any more than they'd take a stroll in the park on a bright Sunday afternoon, their turf was a darker ground more tightly enclosed, rejection Asher said defending it, so there was no question at all of its endurance. I can't go on living like this Asher said, I can't live any other way Devon said, and that was as much dialogue as they ever had about it, Asher putting all such vain hopes out of his head despite wanting before he died to see for himself what beauty was, and truth, and all the other idiocies that'd rung in his child brain; he wouldn't admit what, sometimes, he thought he heard in Devon's harsh music, the noise of a hurt winged primeval creature trying to get off the ground, ambitious to soar but weighted with its own unwieldy mass, in other words as Asher'd say in his treatise on Devon, a compulsive and grotesque impulse to lyricism in spite of itself. There was no life in it otherwise; that may have been why, when Devon set out to compose his self-declared Masterpiece, he wouldn't or couldn't finish it and decided to let the world carry it on for him.

There was no talk, then, no thought of permanence beyond vague plightings of fealty; what would horrify Asher later was to understand that their bond had been no more than a few clumsy words, a few gestures hardly less clumsy, a presumption of love without love's substance: for Asher was unready for anything more, and there were days, nights, when terror followed him around barking at his nerves; time was racing away from him; his life was a farce in which featureless actors galloped through entrances and exits so frenetically that he no longer had any sense of the plot, and behind the crazy humour of it there was a boding of something unaccountably ugly; he thought *If I could only relax, give myself up, accept risk like the grown man I am in a world of risk, then all would be well.* Devon's music roared and rattled in his ears; he thought *No happy man could dream such sounds, why is Devon unhappy, why indeed am I.* Asher was working well, he reminded himself, his careful scribblings were being taken seriously in serious places, he had a constituency who never guessed the emptiness of his heart, he sat on committees and signed petitions, he joined in rallies and demonstrations which in those innocent years still held hope of effect, he was delighted to be sought after, to be busy again after months of aimlessness. He gave Devon credit for recharging him, though Devon himself took no part in these adventures and often derided them, refused to become Political as Asher wanted him to be, laughed at the connections Asher liked to make between his life in public and his life in bed. Petrov also laughed and tried without success to warn Asher that the knots he was so ardently tying were made of frail string, fraying and slipping even as he bound them. Petrov and Asher came close to blows over this and other frictions, and while Asher wouldn't admit it, the end was already beginning.

It wasn't, as people say, that we were growing apart: the gap had always been there, unnoticed or denied. When you attacked me, Petrov, called me insincere, a trifler, you were merely right—and I knew it, that was the hurtful thing, the thing never to be conceded; I made excuses so faint I can't remember now what they were or how I supposed you'd believe them, you taunted me with Joan again and you were right, I'd treated her foully in the name of confusion, as I'd do again in the name of need, meanwhile my famous ideas which people thought so deep were thin as a film, obscuring more than they exposed, and I knew that, too, as I knew my speeches and marches and rancorous meetings were fraudulent, and my celebrations of Devon fraudulent, the whole apparatus of my being was as you didn't neglect to tell me a matchstick scaffolding unable to bear for long the weight of illusion I was piling on it, oh you were absolutely correct, though I pretended it was only jealousy, sour grapes, that moved you to speak, I pretended later it was some will to ruin me that inspired you to bring Devon and Sweetiegirl together, when it was I realize now a will to save me while there was anything humanly salvageable—or salvageably human—left in me, I came near to hating you for that when I ought to have been thanking you, and Devon and I battled that night as if to confirm you, Devon stalking out of the bar leaving me to receive the message he'd not believe until the crunch did finally come down and you, Petrov, against all principle except perhaps friendship, I don't know what it was, you were our rescuer.

I was not to be allowed even that little heroism.

I was not to redeem myself so easily.

But Asher already realized he was in trouble, his life a holding-pattern above some fogged-in airport where nobody, except perhaps Petrov, expected him to land. No emergency vehicles waited on the runway, only silence from the control tower. Fuel running low, passengers beginning to panic, the pilot in a stupor. Public Asher exuded bonhomie, spent energy prodigally, leaned so heavily on his self-deceptions that the sheer weight of his need for them pressed them into the shape of truth. Private Asher was a zombie. "Someday," he promised Petrov and Julie (but not himself), "someday I'll pull out of this." He wondered what the this was. He saw Devon sleek and successful, at peace with Sweetiegirl, all the ruinous past surrendered, the dead buried, the ghosts gone elsewhere. There had been a time, he thought sentimentally, when we actually worked at living, it was a full-time woefully undercompensated job we did for the perverse love of it, now the days come and go with no effort, and this is exactly what we'd always sworn to forbid happening. So it was a surprise to have that past pop up unbidden out of its coffin, altogether alive and more than a little annoyed about its premature interment, to have it barge back into Asher's world without so much as a by-your-leave.

It may be that the truly important events are the ones which don't happen. Life is anticlimax, Asher wrote somewhere. The long-awaited letter opened in fear and trembling contains no more than a casual greeting. The dreaded visitation passes without incident. A lover's disappearance turns out to have a rational explanation. The collapse of an affair is mere misunderstanding, soon mended. Fire trucks scream up to the door; it's a false alarm. The cops aren't looking for you, as you've thought, but for someone with a similar name. With the fuel gauge swinging toward zero, suddenly the fog lifts, radio contact is restored, runway lights come up, the crippled craft touches down like a feather.

Terror, Asher told Petrov once, is possibility, not eventuality.

"You can say that," Petrov answered, "simply because it happens to be true of your life. For the mass of people, terror actually becomes eventuality; things possible to occur do occur, continually. Joan, for instance, really did go mad, really did kill herself, and if you felt no terror then it's nothing to be proud of. Devon murdered somebody—what did he feel? Or you, when you heard about it. There are events in the world, and someday one of them is going to impinge on you, it's going to be right there demanding something of you, chances are you won't be ready for it, you won't know what to do, and all your nice theories won't be a bit of help. The crunch, pal, is only waiting for its moment to fall."

Naturally I believed you.

Because, Petrov, I wanted it to happen. One more blast to blow me out of complacency, out of safety, out of I didn't know what that smothered me, because I'd kidded myself in love, because I'd slipped into a trough of ideas not lived but only thought and thought incompletely, because nothing mattered . . . and if you're confused how much more so was I, whom everyone envied who didn't know me, the contradictions being so many and so incapable of resolution that the last hope was for an explosion to level the whole impossible structure, which I might then rebuild to any better design that presented itself. Your good advice fell on more fertile ground than you suspected, and up grew strange flora indeed, whether healing or poisonous I was never to be sure.

Devon on the run, then. No longer playing rinky-dink in fag clubs, pumping the organ in skidroad missions, humping ivories for small change and beer. Devon with Eli, with Sweetiegirl, with Eli and Sweetiegirl. No longer seedy or sallow, hair razor-cut, styled, actually god help us clean, spiffy new clothes bought with Eli's concert fees, Sweetiegirl's tricks, commissions from the symphony, the opera, the networks. Devon no longer on the run, just a slow trot. Improbably engaged, more improbably married, Sweetiegirl off the streets and into the kitchen of a humble but cozy pseudo bungalow on the west—which is to say the humble-but-comfortable—side of town. Eli on tour, in Europe, in Russia. Civilized arrangements among civilized adults. Reconciliations, an erosion of constraint. We can do it just once more, for old time's sake. No whoopydoo thrill, exactly, but no grief either. Lots of compassion, tact, Sweetiegirl understanding, consenting, Joan trying to understand, coming around, the women now the best of buddies, drinking in smart lounges, going dancing without us, getting into crafts, trading salacious tidbits, thinking of babies, Sweetiegirl ultimately producing one, not necessarily Devon's, Devon magnanimous.

I began work on a treatise on aesthetics, very abstruse, very dull, with peculiar reference, not unprejudiced, to Devon's music, which was becoming semi-well-known. Indeed, you were on your way to being a little bit of a celebrity; composers of putatively Serious music are rare enough birds to be interesting, even and perhaps especially to folks who'd never think of listening to any, and you had immense charm when you saw fit to show it, as you did more often now, you charmed the talk shows, the journalists, everyone loved your wild and raunchy past, which you no longer bothered to deny. All this happened very swiftly, or seemed to.

And Asher, Asher went south.

To remember, chiefly. To summon back things no stain of order could traduce. To rebuild his gutted history.

SPLITTING UP

IN THE MONTHS OF ACCOMMODATING AFTER DEVON left, the first months of Joan, there was no species of contentment I'd not have tried, any accessible satisfaction to dull the rage of days. Slovenly Asher melted in Joan's heat, heartsick Asher gobbled placebos, abandoned work, made excuses to friends unwilling to be hidden from, lay daylong in bed pitying Asher, letting Joan as he thought pity Asher, comprehending nothing of her, seeing nothing of the fear in her, the fear it may have been of a life of Asher, or it may have been the loss of Asher, for that was never not in the wind, he'd never be sure afterwards which of the manifold varieties of fear it had been, they'd never spoken much beyond the ritual unfelt tenderness, imbecilities of the dinner table where they ate well now while Joan's job lasted, but that wasn't for long, and meanwhile Asher blaming Devon and hating daily more dully, more abstractly, meanwhile also wondering why beyond the ordinary glories of bed he could expose toward Joan so little more than the sexual reflex, his ungiving need, selfish Asher utterly ignorant of this woman past the screen of companionableness and sympathy she steadily wore and steadily dreaded more and more the donning of, the bright bright mask that in Asher's vision or lack thereof never slipped, cracked, split open even for a split instant to let him look, if he'd let himself look, into the dark place of the fear, which she guarded for his sake with small talk and smiles, spaghetti dinners, party favours of the bedroom, so that much, much later Asher would curse himself for not having looked in time, but he was a dead man.

Asher recovered, his vision didn't.

He could see Devon again, or risk the possibility of seeing him, without dismay. He could go back without trepidation to the club they'd met in, and see it almost unsentimentally as the greedy and sorrowful dive it was. He rarely left alone, rarely left twice in the same company, and these ventures, hasty and anonymous as he preferred them to be, and utterly irrelevant as he preferred them to be to the world of feeling, no more than a jump and jiggle in the dark, afforded him a kind of mean and chilly triumph, for each of these cocksuckers of convenience, as he thought of them unkindly, was to him another nail in Devon's sexual coffin. A pity, he thought, that Devon wasn't around to watch him now. There came a day when, bored to exasperation with a Student Prince who wanted promises of love eternal and Our Own Little Hideaway (at Asher's expense, it can be presumed), he nailed down the lid and shipped the coffin away, for good.

It had been impossible, of course, to conceal these assignations from Joan, nor had he tried, since the preliminaries had to be negotiated under her expressionless eye as she tended the bar. On this subject she said nothing whatsoever, and Asher for his part was shy to ask; he assumed she must simply be taking the correct and liberated view that his infidelities were no threat to her, no repudiation. When they stopped, she said nothing either.

At this point, there were no people in Asher's world, none at all, and by a freak of fortune it would be Devon himself who, to Asher's appalled surprise, would restore them to him.

As a tepid spring dissolved into a tepid summer, as Asher began cautiously to work again, assembling the detritus of an almost forgotten ambition, after Joan, in a fit of rebellion so outwardly atypical that Asher refused to acknowledge it as real, quit her job and went back to painting the dour, muted canvases that have been much admired lately (though lately is a little too belatedly for Joan), the two of them embarked on a recurring conversation which went on, at classically ordered intervals, with few and minor and finely calculated variations, for the rest of their life together. During his recuperation, if such it was, Asher had found himself watching late movies on television, just as healthy people do, and he'd observed that lovers in late movies, notably those of the articulate past, were mysteriously competent to talk. Not, to be sure, that what they said was profound or poetic or to any degree original, more often it was as witless and hysterical as life itself, but it was, for all its cheapness, more talk than Asher and Joan had had since the night he'd thrown himself witless and hysterical at her door and on her mercy, and he considered that inasmuch as words were his sole trade he ought to be able, was morally obliged, to expend a few of them on his mate, and she on him. He wasn't expecting much, he certainly wasn't up to elevated discourse, but now that his mind was (as he supposed, fool) clearing itself of Devon, he reckoned he could spare a few well-chosen sentences now and then from the horde he still proposed to commit to paper.

The subject he chauvinistically chose for the dialogue, without prior consultation re Joan's preferences, was Splitting Up.

People in movies, as we all know, are forever splitting up; uncelluloid people Asher and Joan knew were doing the same; they themselves had attempted it a number of times and occasionally had succeeded; what Asher proposed was to *take forever* splitting up. The split itself would be the first and final principle, but it would be permitted to remain unacted in the universe of principles, uncontaminated by anything as gauche as having happened. It would be happening. As process it would be intellectually tenable and, if managed at a moderate pace, emotionally gripping but not too exhausting; it would satisfy most of the open-n-honest quotas of the enlightened world; it could, if done right, lead to wonderfully time-killing digressions into psychology, sociology, metaphysics, epistemology, ethics, aesthetics, anthropology, political theory, sexology, theology, autobiography, gossip, and sheer viciousness, from all of which Asher expected them both to derive rare insights and useful conclusions, with fringe bonuses in the amusement of their friends and the confusion of their enemies, who in turn could engage spare hours of their own in a similar pursuit. The idea could snowball, Asher thought. It could breed compassion, as acquaintances enquired about the current status of the splitting. It could supply material for students of drama, writers in all genres, media, tax brackets; it could create jobs for surplus statisticians. Men and women, gay couples, pairs of all persuasions frustrated by the customary speech dryup of familiarity would now have something to say that would never lose interest. Asher, broaching the notion with what he hoped was the suitable level of candor, *I'm gonna fuck off out of this stinking house*, felt a messianic exaltation that so amply irrigated his arid spirit that he began to weep almost immediately, loudly, thereby missing Joan's murmured answer, *Why don't you do that very thing, tonight for example?*

Devon, Joan, I have an apology to make, or more accurately an accounting. The first item of which is that I don't remember and can't invent what I said to you when I was saying dreadful things in my folly, and this is not a failure of imagination or desire but one of faith, because Asher at his most hungry was all the time unfaithful to faith, and was a weak and silly man the more you thought him strong and earnest, and the stronger and earnester you thought him the stronger and earnester he presumed and pretended to be, all the while melting in alien warmths I couldn't keep lit, not for the life of me; and when I was most cold I wanted to eat something sustaining, when most hot, I wanted to fast, got everything backwards whatever I did and the cruel instrument Mind worked overtime without compensation to cheat Asher of his memories guilt absolution words. You never didn't know I was faking.

You split.

What happened, finally, is best gotten over with right now. Asher and Joan spent most of a year, or a week, or however long it took, a period Asher never did measure with any accuracy, applying his theory and finding it inadequate. During the experiment, Joan went on serving him seamlessly; the erosion didn't impinge on him; the comedy of their misery was irresistibly watchable; spectators gradually understood that, as long as the play was in progress, they were relieved of any responsibility for their own shaky couplings. So Asher thought, marvelling as he railed at Joan that she never once flinched at the railing, that no tears of hers ever noticeably dampened the famous pillow the presumed dampness of which had all their friends engrossed. *We can't go on like this*, Asher'd say serenely, and Joan'd say, *You're right, we can't*, and he'd think how reasonable she is, how *simpatico*, and she'd think something, perhaps about the canvas waiting to be darkened with its sprawled images of mud, blood, broken pillars, hooded black figures in tableaux which to Asher suggested atavistic rites. *Our relationship is unhealthy*, he reminded her, hugging her on his way to the bar, and Joan, who by then was pals with Sweetiegirl, everyone trying his, her or its damnedest to be civilized, went out that night to another bar with her and said, *Asher thinks we're unhealthy. What do you think?* I think, Sweetiegirl answered, that there's a big difference between being unhealthy and being sick. Figure it out.

Sweetiegirl, who had a formidably retentive memory and a mouth that retained nothing, repeated their whole exchange to Asher some months thereafter, under the impression that she was doing him a favour. To possess privileged knowledge in bad times is like having a surplus case or two of beer on a Canadian Sunday: you don't need it for yourself, so how can you decline to share it? *Of course* you'll share it; and Sweetiegirl, into whose selves Joan in her extremity poured more of her heart than she'd previously guessed she had, succeeded wonderfully at telling Asher the Compleat Shit the complete shit, which had he not been sequestered in his own mania he could have known for himself without the telling. What hurt most, in all the forthcoming rhapsody of hurt, was that Asher and Sweetiegirl were in bed at the time, he having done a sloppy job of pleasing her, she at the moment of his coming having made a spontaneously foul remark about his needing a Cock Traffic Controller, at which point the flying object went down not in flames but in the sticky muck he'd wake in tomorrow. That, Sweetiegirl said, was a whimper not a bang, whereupon began the recitation of Asher's sins, which continued hours past the indeterminate moment when for want of anything more unaccustomed to do he fell asleep.

Take this part slowly.

Asher'd heard, in a vague way, that Devon had appropriated some of his notes and journals and chicken scratchings, the sort of inchoate stuff aspiring writers leave lying around, and had for his own presumably vengeful reasons used them to pad his latest opera. Letters, not awfully informative, were exchanged. There was something about a commission, something subsequently about a decommission, problems with the score, the libretto, the laws of libel, the Musicians Union, the insurmountable technical difficulties of staging eternity; it was all quite unclear to Asher, who had insurmountable technical difficulties of his own to deal with: face it, he wasn't all that interested. Slowly, Asher.

THE PO-HOY-NICKS

ALL RIGHT. SLOWLY. YOU SPLIT. I DID THE TALKING, you did nothing. There was a job open on one of the islands, you took it. In a hotel. It was, you said, a chance to get out from under. The Tides Inn. To get your head, little pieces of which had been chipping off like dandruff, together.

You neglected to wash the dishes before I drove you to the boat. You neglected to take with you the leather coat I helped you steal; it was too large for you, anyway. You neglected to mention a great many small but intrusively significant business matters that you'd always taken care of and I didn't know the first thing about. You neglected to mention, Joan my love, that you planned to come back.

The first time I ever went to the Tides Inn, long before I knew you, I was wiped on acid. We sat on the veranda drinking beer, Petrov and I. The sun was shining, monotonously, on the sea. There was a problem about the fishboats: how many of them were there, out on the sea, beyond the veranda, with the October sun slurping down on them? *How many fucking fishboats, Petrov?* I see three. But they keep moving around. Which is the one I counted last? I see three, six, twelve, a million fishboats, out there, in the blazing blue sea, going around and around for no reason. On one of them a woman is making notes for the novel she'll write about being, or having been, a cook on a fishboat. Which one, Petrov? This is terrifically important, and all you can do is sit there looking historical, with your beer and your beard, the trouble with you being, Pet, that you never in your whole delicately modulated life got wiped *anything*, much less wiped out, least of all on acid, that's LSD-25, look it up sometime in the pharmacology or whatever, just tell me *how many goddamn christly fucking fishboats*, out there, in the amazing sea . . . . Don't you understand it's an epistemological issue?

Along with the three overstuffed red horsehair chairs, Joan left me a cardboard box stuffed with the books I'd bought to educate her with, and a coffee table painted in her style: a tired Phoenix, preferring ashes over air. The Po-hoy-nicks, she pronounced it. Will it rise? she asked. Eh? Will it soar, up up and away?

How many fishboats?

It rose, the Po-hoy-nicks, it rose and flew, it flew, it flew, before it fell. But ashes are warm, soft, a bed treasonable to leave. There was the night Joan fell off the desk, trying to change a light bulb to prove she could do it, Joan standing on the same stupid desk I write at now, wobbling, the cat barking somewhere in another room, and Joan was waving there with one hand up to screw the bulb into the socket, which was just slightly in the wrong place, a little over to the left, that's right, so she fell *oh shit* on top of me, a weight of breakage collapsing me. The bulb broke and hissed in a corner, insulted. Joan was wearing one of those red velvet things that pass for clothes, in the circles I don't encircle. We might as well fuck, she said, now that we're here on the fucking floor.

Johnny? Are you reading this? Over my shoulder, hanging on me like a Fat Lady's furs? *Look, I'm not being moralistical or nothing, you do what you fucken want, but this street's no fucken place.* How do I know? Because I was there, sweetheart, I was there before you were fucken born, lover, I played piano in a ratshit bar, and the queers came up and put money in the fucken piano so I'd play Their Song, and we've fucken heard this a million times already and don't fucken want to hear it again but you, Johnny, you, you, you were only an itch in daddy's crotch when I was doing this, and I lay wet beside Joan and said, Sorry, it won't fly. A conundrum or something: in such seas should I drown. The Po-Hoy-Nicks is grounded. We walk across the airstrip. Devon and Asher—no, wait, we'd had a drink first in an expensive hotel, I was just normally sweating and stinking, and I wouldn't know until two hours later whether you'd given me the syph. Devon said, If I ever catch you screwing anybody but me, I'll fucken murder him, her, or it. So all Asher's friends got the syph. From him. It stands to reason.

Johnny, don't come back tonight. You're younger than I ever was and have more strength. You'll make it just fine in the street. Go to Calgary and get rich. Go out stealing. Love, and do what you will, and I never knew you, never—

Joan neglected to wash the dishes before I drove her to the boat. Scum of remembered roast beef on the plates. Third-world *haute cuisine*. She fell from the desk to the tirelessly accommodating floor, and said, We might as well.

Fuck.

I don't know the mechanics of the body. All this extraordinary network of stuff is what manages to remember you, speak to you, when you wake up beside it later. Breathe hard, Petrov, this is the steamy part. I don't know how it works. All this, forgive me, being is wrapped around you in our dirty bed on the floor or upside down in the bathtub, who gives a shit, all this is just you tying my legs around yours, legs for fucksake, you'd never have thought the poor pins we walk on would mean so much, is that a toe? A foot? One of them items what makes footsteps? In the sands of? I don't fucken care if you haven't washed it since last week at the VD clinic. Is that an ankle? You can't fool me, you were wearing the wool socks to make it look thick, strong, a pillar, huh? To hold up what? And that calf, there, that one, yeah, the one I'm slopping my tongue down, the curve of it that's yours alone, distinguishing it—oh shut up let me have my jokes—from the calves of cows, so that the knees grip the chin being gripped the knees that have, built into themselves, a kind of gentle memory of what to do when, summoned so precipitately, the mouth remembers what to do and does it, the thighs behind spreading soft and warm like the ashes from outta which no Po-hoy-nicks will bother to lift its pitiful wings and rise, sail, fly, go free on the errant currents of the air, while you hold me with . . . .

I said to it, Leave me in peace. Alone, for a change. In The Tides Inn, Petrov said, We haven't any hope. We think right but everything we do is wrong. We don't think right enough, I said. The fishboats circle the remarkable sea. I hate the world for being informative in this way.

Above the knees, the thighs. Simple hinges make the legs move. Thighs are a luxury. Gravy in the bodily boat. I could put my hands on them and they'd squish away. Is there room enough between them for my head then? Do I have to eat the hairs too? I'll think of your hair as spaghetti. You can be the meatball.

It astonished Asher, as it should, that he wanted to take Joan to the boat, that he wanted to stand on the dock when the boat pulled out, that he, who persistently fled into pain only to give himself the thrill of running out on it, should have wanted to stand there on the rotting dock letting somebody run out on him. He could've stopped her. There was time. He could have decided against suggesting they have lunch with Leon and Susan, that perfectly married entity, en route. Leon's the sort of guy who, believing in ceremony per se but rejecting the formats of the traditional ceremonies, says Grace at the table by reading the entire text of Songs of Experience. Blake we didn't need, Joan and I, just then. Susan's the sort of guy who interrupts the ceremony to point out that, since Blake's a notorious sexist, we'd better get on with the moussaka, which is getting cold. I spent this time looking closely at Joan's face, which had high cheekbones, eyes of a reflective colour unsusceptible to description, a peculiarly mobile nose, and the barest wisp of a moustache. It made Asher uncomfortable to think that Devon, too, had that wispy sort of moustache. But had he, who'd always redesigned people to fit his desires of them, *seen* her?

Boats passed in the bay, there was still time if we needed it, we did, but there wasn't time. Susan was saying something about children, how they cement a couple, I thought of Joan and me embedded in this grey clinging gloop, her hip being welded to my thigh, both of us struggling to detach our arms from their tangle, our limbs and organs and all the rest of the taken-for-granted human machinery grinding to a liedown, the archaeologists of the future finding us inexplicably intact like Easter Island heads, cemented by children, condemned to mythology—oh, Asher, you cocksucker, don't you know that everyone's cemented somehow, that the movement of time (there's another boat at six, you can catch it) is just a labour of slugging through thickening cement, we're bound fast, no lesser concrete than Leon and Susan, their children and antiques, fucking jesus they want to come with us to the boat, they demand to be there on the dock with me to make sure I'm all right after you walk out the gangplank and the goddamn Princess of Fuckall sails off into the—and we can't let them do it, not to us, haven't we heard what the road to hell is paved with and there's paving stones all over this house what we gotta do now love is thank the nice people for the nice lunch and embrace warmly fondly cry a little and get our fucking asses out to that fucking car and I'm sorry I'm not being as nice as they are but I don't want you to go and if that asshole says one more word about the lineaments of Gratified Whatever I'll throw the fucking moussaka in his fucking perfectly perfect married face and then I'll have lost you, Joan, because you're nice, too, slowly, Asher, there's still time . . . .

Good-bye good-bye good-bye take care see you have a nice time good luck you too *Joan let's go.*

See you I did, in a green glade twelve miles and as things developed fewer minutes from the dock. I think we were trespassing. Again Asher can't remember; he went back once to look at the place, because it was the only time you ever took me that I didn't take you, though I didn't know then and don't know it now, we parked the car somewhere down the road so obscure that we missed the six o'clock looking for the spot and had another hour on the rotting dock waiting for the seven, but when Asher went back merely to be there again he couldn't find the green glade or the crushed leaves of the trees that witnessed us, he couldn't find the words to remember you, the imprint of cheekbones and buttocks, but what the hell we were saying good-bye and I would, in my fashion, radio on high and the borrowed car dying under my hand, in my fashion, and I'd get there safe and sound and you'd get into your island too, you'd sling drinks to a better class of scum than you'd slung them to in that shithole I met Devon in, the boat steaming out you waving me waving then jesus it was just us I had to drive forty miles back not stopping to be loved in vain by Leon and

Susan and you were going gone, and I knew that I'd been biding my time.

When Joan came back from the island, Asher didn't know what to do. She'd made money, she'd been variously screwed in various ways, she was ready to resume the act they'd collaborated in. It was going to be different this time, they said, Asher having abandoned theory and Joan practice.

NO

EVASIVE ASHER CAN'T SCOURGE HIMSELF TO SAY what's demanding to be said, cowardy custard's stalling again, certain that between the day of Joan's return and the day of the end there were good times, there was *something* wasn't there? that I can resurrect without shame, without terror of making real what all these years I've insisted on the unreality of; Joan, when you came back to me it was you asking for mercy and I withheld it.

I installed you in a motel room, in a world of vinyl and plasterboard for which you never suspected Eli was paying, you trembled all the while we lay together under the acoustic tile beside the wallboard printed to look like imitation knotty pine, you by then had mysterious devouring diseases no doctor could define, I bought you pills from Devon's horde, do I have to tell you I was relieved to leave your bed, happy to walk out and home to the mob I'd conscripted to take your place, travellers who'd quit me more coldly than you did, who'd leave as coldly as I, still unseeing, extracted myself from your need, dressed, snuck out; during all this time Asher tried to think up little things to amuse Joan, to distract her: drives in the country, movies, concerts, picnics, unlikely and unaffordable gifts she looked at bleakly and gave away to chambermaids. People praised what they presumed to be his kindness, his patience, pity, Asher saddled with burdened by bound to, though these rites of attention were really no big deal and introduced into his movements a kind of order he found even pleasurable in its novelty; he'd never concede what was actually the case, that Joan in distress existed no more for him than she had in placid submission; when the motel room yielded as it would into a nuthouse ward he visited punctiliously, smuggling in booze and dope and smuggling out the good behaviour pills that had caused her to lose her hair and looks; improved, as it seemed, she was allowed to roam the hospital grounds at will, watched only by eyes more vacant than her own, and they tried to revive themselves by cheap stratagems, screwing for instance in the back of his car, behind the gymnasium, but there was no pang in it, and without any spoken decision they abandoned the practice. After that his visits became more irregular, briefer, more uncomfortable to anticipate and easier to forget, then they ceased altogether. Then Joan began phoning Asher daily, at hours cunningly chosen for their inconvenience, rambling through thickets of delusion through which he felt obliged, however mapless, to follow; her relentlessly nattering voice was a radio permanently tuned in his head; it struck him that Joan in her craziness had taken possession of him as she'd never been able to do in her sanity; when psychiatrists forbade the calls he was nonetheless unable to silence her, and the softly raving, merciless voice was to dog his inner ear long after he learned from Sweetiegirl that Joan, released under guard on a weekend pass, and judged sufficiently rehabilitated to go to the Ladies unaccompanied, had, in this fashion in the ordinary Friday night confusion of the beer parlour to which she'd begged implacably to be taken, eluded her companion, taken a cab to Asher's, left a note he'd study for three days without comprehending, taken another cab to the beach, and vanished permanently, as Sweetiegirl put it in her inimitable style, into that night where all vanishings are permanent.

May our sins be all forgiven.

What is grief that I don't know if I felt it or not? Devon held me and I wept, of course, weeping's easy to do at the end of things, but how's the isolate spirit to identify these tears as genuine, this feeling as anything as common, as familiar as what the world calls grief? It was still possible to think brutally that in the last weeks I'd probably have hoped for just this solution had its probability occurred to me; I'd so little fathomed Joan that I'd never seriously imagined her capable of any act so definitively punishing, so confusing to such poor sense of her as I had. The record would be blurred forever now: she was safe enough, but her precipit departure had thrown us survivors into a jeopardy far worse than her life itself had done at its most hazardous. I was angry, I felt unfairly used, put upon, stuck with one more block of inexpiable guilt when surely I'd had my portion already. At home I felt oppressed by jettisoned evidences of Joan, her abandoned clothes, furniture, paintings, for the canvases were mine now, a wall of accusations I hadn't wit to read in time. And I was troubled by Devon's readiness to comfort me, to assume that naturally I'd want comforting, that it was his job and right to supply it, that what I was going through was a territory accessible to him, perhaps to anyone, whereas it was in truth inaccessible even to me. I let him hold me and pat me like a wounded puppy, saying obviously unbelievable things like It's not your fault, she didn't know what she was doing, but it was I who hadn't known, hadn't seen, hadn't cared to look, hadn't loved. So I raved at Devon that love was a lie, as it may indeed be, and I summoned from impoverished memory everything mean and gross and ungiving in all of us, I charged all of us with every crime I could name (and god knows the list was long enough to occupy a night), I beseeched Devon to beat me until I bled from nose and mouth, to fuck me in the ass because I'd always hated that and feared him in his moods to do it, and he did it until I bled from there, too, and in the course of those hours I committed Joan to rest and myself to restlessness, and Devon for a second time died in me.

Petrov the Arranger took care of the arrangements, identified the body when it washed up, answered the questions, signed the papers, organized the burial. Though Joan to no one's knowledge had ever been in the least religious, he unaccountably decided on a more or less orthodox Christian service, which was apparently allowable because having been officially incompetent of mind she wasn't answerable for her suicide; all this was determined through muted telephone consultations to which I tried not to listen; at least he managed to rustle up a church and clergy hospitable to his importunities, and we buried Joan on a day of brilliant light and blazing heat with all the arid pomp of faith not a one of us felt for a single fucking moment.

Abide with me, the rented choir intoned. *I am the Resurrection and the Life*, the rented reverend intoned. That's odd, I thought, Joan certainly wouldn't have gone for that, nor do I now. I wondered why Petrov, passionate Marxist that he was and is, Petrov who'd never liked Joan or condoned my choice of her, who much more than I had been party to and agent of her committal, Petrov whose trust was altogether in history not in the pieties of eschatology and whose millennium would come by the gun if it came at all—I wondered why Petrov had gone to so much trouble for Joan. Perhaps he also wondered. At the pauper's graveside I stood between Devon and Sweetie-girl while the coffin went down and Eli sang unaccompanied a requiem of Devon's last-minute inspiration; we were in a semicircle holding hands and I had to war against an awful laughter because our lives had been and would continue to be as pointlessly pathetic as Joan's death and this was no shit-hot revelation after all, it hadn't a shred of its vaunted dignity to redeem it, it was just a shabby little fact in a universe of shabby little facts, and I could remember with screaming clarity when Joan had been if not beautiful at least acceptably pretty and quick and warm to forgive, and I'd thoughtlessly taken that and eroded it to ratshit, let nobody ever say I had no choice, let nobody ever say I couldn't have helped myself and her if I'd had even one grain of moral vision, but no mea culpas were gonna change what had happened, everybody knows that, so what the funereal fuck are we supposed to be doing standing here weeping and gnashing and feeling eversosorry for ourselves, and Eli's voice at that instant, straining for a cruelly high E beyond his powers, wavered and cracked and he began to giggle then howl with laughter, which was contagious and swept through us like an epidemic, incurable as life itself or love itself if love there be, and that forgive me was how it came to pass that Joan entered upon eternity to the sound of merriment.

Well, Petrov old man, it could be true as you say that we're all victims of history, histories of oppression threading through every life alive, I won't deny that though it's awfully easy to say and for some of us harder to prove than it may be for you, but even granting its measure of truth for argument's sake I'm still not one hundred per cent convinced it was history Joan was a victim of. Devon, yes, now I can see that, at least it's fairly demonstrable up to a point, what with poverty and crime and the collapse of justice and the impossibility of justice and so forth, Devon surely would have been your classic history-victim but for one thing, his music, and so might I too but for one thing, which you're holding in your hands right now; but Joan, no, I won't quite concede that yet. You're invited to refuse me. Unless we're to blame the action of history for the meagreness of our hearts' means, unless we proclaim, as no doubt you would, that our passions are as governable by material cause as our choice of an automobile or an insurance policy, then we have to look elsewhere for Joan's killer, and on this subject, Petrov my pet, I have rather more to ask than to answer. Now I have never been, as you perfectly well know, a religious man of any sort, nor am I, as I bloody well hope you know, weakening in my dotage, so it is therefore with the greatest trepidation and trembling that I venture upon these matters, not to say We are Fallen, which I emphatically fail to believe, nor to submit that the unholiness of the heart's affections can be sloughed off on theological grounds however sentimentally appealing such a cop-out may loom at times, nor to propose that some dispensation of grace or commission of penitence might yet excuse us our murders as, to give an example close to home, Devon's though legally "pardoned" at last were not excused either by himself or by the thugs who came to take him—but Petrov, tell me, is there another sense of excuse possible to us without softening of the brain, or are we condemned to remain unexcused and unexcusable for eternity?

Now that Joan's gone, and let's not kid ourselves that she was effectively gone long before the water swallowed her, now that Joan's gone, you said on the way home from the funeral, there's no good reason not to get on with the things that matter. You didn't name them, of course, we knew what they were. What you didn't say but certainly thought was that Joan had never been, for any of us really, among the things that mattered: had she been, she might have survived. My responsibility for her was not taken, not acted upon as it demanded, not lived.

Perhaps I should just stop here. Perhaps it's not given to us to live responsibility according to the puffed-up notions we like to entertain about it when we're not required to do anything about it; you, Petrov, would insist to the death that otherwise quite unremarkable fallible fucked-up people do it as if automatically all the time, so why couldn't we, why can't we now? You'd tell me that when I hid Devon from his avengers I was, for the first time in your knowledge of me, acting deliberately on a principle of faith intelligible to you—that it was the first time I did something right, even if, at that point and maybe ever since, you felt constrained to query my motives, Devon having what you correctly called an Unhealthy Power over me; shit yes, that was plain enough, and no ground for argument. But what, by comparison, did Joan ask of me? To see her as she was? Really? What good would me seeing have done her if I'd offered it? When I was with her, you said in one breath that I exploited her (sure I did), in another that she also was using me, though for what was never very clear. Her body was an anaesthetic to quiet the pain of Devon, to which end I have to admit it never wholly succeeded; her very forcelessness was balm to a rawness that asked a stronger medicine: wasn't *she*, mad or not, a partner to my folly?

I will wonder about this, Petrov, all my days.

Oh wasn't the world lovely and innocent in your unquestioning arms, Joan, the only place it was, and didn't I know that and deny it each time your legs opened to me and your eyes filmed with what I said to myself had to be happiness, weren't those sweaty nights and long afternoons our cut-rate purchase of heaven, costume heaven though it was, weren't our brays of pleasure better music than any Devon would live to compose, when we were strong in our rich foolishness and dreamed of fighting history side by side, indestructible in love, and we befriended Petrov at a march to protest I forget what, he spoke poetry and truth unto us, telling us more than we'd ever thought tellable about the Things that Matter, which did matter dreadfully, and you were a painter and I was a lover dilly-dilly, we'd be king and queen of the New Dispensation wherein it'd make no difference which of us was which.... This was before I met Devon, who as we fucked and marched and sang and dreamed ourselves changing the world was being Underground as we never truly could be. Devon slipping sneaking slithering from house to house on his way to us, what had he done anyway but blow up a mailbox so that the only crime he'd ever be caught at was done not for principle or polity but for cash to buy junk, Devon hitchhiking hopping freights stealing his way across the dismal continent toward the moment when, desperate for bread, he'd swallow pride and take a gig playing rinky-dink in the queer club where Joan, her head unknown to me a gallery of violent dark pictures, had taken to barkeeping to pay the rent on our costly studio, to pay the dope the dues the duty on me. Asher, then, edited a small journal of intransigent opinion, much of it more Petrov's than his own, which lost readership and money steadily as its constituency aged and lost heart. Asher went to meetings at which he was vigorously abused for dissolutions real and imaginary, for deviances he'd never suspected himself of, for his persistent reluctance to accept correctness for its own sake; and after one of these sessions he either resigned or was purged, he couldn't determine which because both things seemed to be happening simultaneously. Petrov, for the record, stood by him despite having much to sacrifice by so doing. Without the journal and the meetings to anchor him, Asher became restless, querulous, more introspective than was good for him, and impotent. In a fit of causeless rancour he moved out of Joan's studio and into a dilapidated communal shack with Petrov, Julie, their kids, an army deserter fugitive under the name of Victor Red, Lisa, the overindulged sixteen-year-old daughter of a dissident nuclear physicist of some renown, Marty, the guru of a curious cult, and an ever-changing procession of fair folk whose names and origin and pursuits and passions were to Asher a graph of the age, which as we remember was an age of false promises and fickle visions and deceptions which gleamed like misplaced lighthouses on a landlocked prairie. Here amid cockroaches and tame mice, dope fumes, dialectics and dust Asher lived on welfare and wrote poetry even he realized stank, and stank himself, and prayed for an apocalypse to settle the score once and for all.

If I'd seek an image for this time, it might be a painted-over mirror into which I peered vainly in search of the face, my own, which couldn't be reflected. The original nature of the object said *This is a mirror*, but nothing could any longer be mirrored in it. Petrov and I sniffed each other's minds like prurient pups, all the while neutered in our hearts (or wherever the seat of action is). Any insignificant detail of life assumed enormous importance in direct proportion to its insignificance—the less consequential an obsession, the more it defended us, or me at least, against the huge obsessions we were, or I was, in flight from. An hour's debate with Julie over dishwashing duty was an hour forbidden to darker contemplations; the shrieks and cries of the rigorously self-improving downstairs drowned out the noises of intolerable thought; Victor Red's stateless plight was somehow proof against the still larger and lonelier statelessness to which we were all, however variously and vicariously, committed.

Lies and bullshit. What the fuck was *wrong* then? Asher thought he'd have all the time to correct his mistakes, that's why he made them prodigally without a second spared for consequence, that's why when he supposed himself to have escaped he became Asher again, hollow, why when Devon smoked into his life Asher was ready for him, in degradation if nothing else equal to him, to the world that both of them knew as enemy. Our language was not equal. To the task, Petrov, our language wasn't equal. "We have to get it together," you said, for example. (See, I remembered the quotation marks.) Get exactly what together, old buddy? Red Victor, as we ended up calling Victor Red, had a better sense than we did of what had to be done: in the middle of the night, he stole a boat and set sail for Russia, the coast of which he saw luminous across uncrossable waters, all you had to do was point the bow in a direction obscurely northwest of here and with any luck the current would carry you there. The current with expectable luck carried him to a marina where he beached the boat and several others, and hitchhiked home. Yet wasn't there a moment, of course there was a moment, when, alone in the black harbour in the inevitable rain, without fuel or compass or any sort of chart beyond his own thinking, Victor saw Russia, lived the triumphant hour of his arrival there (what seas how bravely negotiated, what storms passed through, what privations overcome), the commissars massed on the dock to welcome him, honour him, decorate him for seizing the vision the rest of us merely talked about .... I thought him mad, as I thought so many mad whose curse it was to see more lucidly, at last, than I.

The man who fell to you, Devon, The Victim as the papers would name him, I used to see him around the bars, I knew his bad business, what did he think, or you, at the instant of the reckoning? Inconceivable, is it, that such a one could think at all? What hatreds you bore I never asked; possibly I had enough of my own to enquire into. Scum, you'd say, leaving the matter there, by no intentional irony in the same word Asher's family reserved for his ill-chosen childhood cronies, but we must suppose that this particular scum had sufficient brain left, before the pain and blessed blackness took it over, to look into your appalled, boyish face as you stood watching him, stood for just the briefest second paralyzed with knowledge, not yet thinking of escape, the necessary deceptions, the eventually unavoidable retributions.

Meanwhile I drifted through that time in love with listlessness, debating with Petrov, suspended, sometimes seeing Joan sometimes working at not seeing her, getting myself arrested on principle and released on bail the origins of which I didn't ask, talking revolution with Victor Red and Jesus with Julie who'd accepted him much as she'd accepted me; it astonishes me to recall how we lived, that we lived at all, as if every day were eternity and time itself had no direction but was as spongy and shapeless an element as the mattresses we variously shared; strange as it seems this was the only period in my memory when I was actually selfless, without identity or purpose, wanting none, writing down as though by rote the cheap brilliances which would one day make Asher's small reputation and smaller fortune, sleeping and screwing and walking nowhere in a city as featureless as I where everything was only and always what its familiarity said it was, holding Joan's damp hand saying *You're right I never loved you, you're right I wouldn't recognize love if it came right up and spat in my face*, which finally it did.

That night—that night, Devon, I'd been thinking about Order, how so many better minds than mine had expended so much attention to the pursuit of it, the care and feeding of it, the protection of the myth of it: for I recognized no order in myself, just massive fucking shapelessness, nor any in the world either for that matter, though people went on driving automobiles up and down streets according to signs and lights—*directions*, Devon—and stories on television had plots that began at the beginning and sailed obliviously through the middle straight to the end and I myself composed orderly sentences which English teachers would subsequently dote upon as models of grammar and syntax and the government sent me and I duly scribbled upon questionnaires which presumed that I truly knew the answers to the huge and lunatic questions they asked and the price of beer rose according to economic laws as the price of experience fell according to more inscrutable laws, and *there was no Order anywhere Devon no Order in any of what looked most orderly*, this despite centuries yea eternities of thought applied to the subject by men and women of deep probity and rigour, qualities I surely lacked, Devon, the more I coveted them, Order being infucking-comprehensible to this no-longer-kid who nevertheless continued to get out of bed and through the days and streets to Joan's club, your terrible piano-playing, urgent bodies fighting off empty dawn, your eyes grabbing me—me, of all people, so that for a split heartbeat there was, if not Order, some perverse imitation of the dream of Order, some notion so spectacularly irrational that to this day I shudder to admit it before the world, that what I'd been living was not life but might yet be and you poor fucker were to be the unsuspecting instrument of this birth just because you had the hard luck to be there and in your wasted way beautiful and in your unstated need available to me, it could have been anyone and better no doubt had it been, but I was thinking of the Soul that unimaginable creature and how it was altogether probably that I didn't have one, you'd provide one if I had to drag it out of your body screaming, cocksucker you'd call me but it wasn't your cock I was sucking, trust old Asher to have a loftier ambition than the lowly incongruous genitals, on second thought my darling don't trust him, he never trusted himself and for good reason too . . . .

It is some time later, a few hours or days, when Devon phones, needing bread, a place to go, of course. Asher knowing what he wants.

May all our sins be forgiven.

I WENT TO SEE JOAN

I WENT TO SEE JOAN. WHEN SHE CALLED, FINALLY, Devon took the phone, handed it to me with a sacrificial shrug: I told you so, his face said. Joan, he mouthed, holding the receiver to his breastbone. Devon looked more wolfish than ever, his narrow predatory face fixed. We see people as if in medieval caricatures: we still believe in physiognomy. As a man looks so is he. The face of the monster was always the face of the god. Sacrifices were made to such as you, when you were Pallas Athena, glinting like the gilded tower of bank buildings off the shields of an army of lovers—

I almost said I'm not here, tell her I'm not here.

Take the fucking phone, said Devon, I wondered which of us he was feeling contempt for; the stink of contempt was in the room. I thought of saying: I'm not here, please tell her I'm not here. In the park, they were singing

True blue
To you I give my aw-aw-awll.

It might have been true, might as well have been. All the way up the hill, going home, Asher imagined what it must have been like to have lived young in such a place. Where everybody knew about everybody. The moment you were born your safe death was guaranteed you. All you had to do, to qualify for it, was get through the years between. Make money, wait, be nice. All you had to do was agree, in a gentlemanly way, to the gentleman's agreement.

I could sense Devon behind me, spot-jogging, snuffling hungrily, watching me with that kind of stepped-on eagerness that seems to carry out the threat of physical assault in the act of refusing it. "You never trusted me," Joan said. "You never thought I had what it took to know what you go about claiming you know." I said something quick and indifferent into the phone, something businesslike, like you weren't flesh of my flesh, bone of my bone. I'd do anything now to arrange a time, a place. Call it Her Place.

In a country we never had the grace to live in, there was a rebellion against the mystery of myth. To paint what you saw, as opposed to what you were told to be aware of, was the heresy. Every act of desire, of recognition, was to be made crazy. These lights, when I lift my eyes to them, are not the photocarbons which guide expensive machinery across viaducts to taverns and whorehouses and exotic restaurants. They sing to me when I walk home at night. They shine like shining does, against the darkness.

Immediately the thought that Joan had a place of her own, hers solely, as yet unfamiliar to me, was wrenching in a way I hadn't expected: it meant you really were still alive, still functioning without me. "That wasn't part of our bargain," Asher said. "You were supposed to die when I said you would. People who trust the evidence of the senses to portray conditions of insensibility can be forgiven for failing to look at the scenery."

I'm hanging up, we said, in near-unison.

"It's all right," Devon whispered before Asher had a chance to speak to him. "Honestly, it's all right. She's only gonna want money, anyway." He put his arm around me. Devon's face was carved to register suffering beautifully.

Automatically I said, I haven't got any.

The apartment was one of many in a big, shabby, stuccoed-over house on a street doomed to rehabilitation. A mild reek of Lost Generation poetry in the stairwell. A furnished bed-sitting-room with a rusty sink and a leatherette hide-a-bed; a kitchen, sort of, in what had been a closet. Cracked flowered linoleum, a thin braided rug over it. Ridiculously, a picture of me tacked to the wall, one of Devon's early masterpieces, so mendaciously lighted that I looked almost presentable, lean and brooding instead of skinny and sad.

You came, Joan said.

For once.

Funny. I guess you'll want a drink.

She'd gained weight, colour, looked older, what's the word?—matronly. In a bedspread-print caftan, rouge and lipstick and powder applied with the studied seriousness of somebody who'd never got used to wearing makeup. I've seen novice transvestites, fat boys on a first trip out, decorated like that. Once, at a party in a semi-chic Hollywood restaurant, where what I had in common with the other guests was that we all wondered what I was doing there, an ample movie star a few character parts past her prime came over and offered me a slice of pizza. I wasn't hungry. The famous motherly face bubbled and collapsed. I made the fucking pizza myself, you don't want any? And I thought, brilliantly, my god, they're human too.

I sat on the hide-a-bed, drank expensive scotch out of a coffee mug, edited the news, stared at Joan so fiercely she had to say, at one point, You're angry. You're still angry.

I wasn't. I said, I don't know what I am.

He won't stay with you. Meaning Devon.

I know that. I knew; she didn't have to remind me. I felt a swift thirst the whisky couldn't quench, got up, filled my glass with water from the grey and red sink, gulped it down, refilled, gulped again. Wiped my mouth slobbily, poured more scotch. These movements had the loaded stateliness of sacrament. Look, I said, why did you want to see me?

I wanted to see you. Surely we can still . . . talk?

But that's just what we can't do. We're not doing it.

When Devon left, the first time, I set out to find him, and did. It was early in the morning and I'd stayed up all night waiting for the liquor store to open so I could get a bottle to hit him with if he wouldn't drink it with me. I had a notebook full of eloquent things to say; I'd even written his own lines into the script. God knows how I figured out which hotel he'd be in. Maybe he told me. Another time. Before. Or let it be instinct, but I have noticed that in some kinds of crisis there's a species of knowledge that transmits itself unbidden through unofficial channels. So I found him, right where I didn't stop to think he wouldn't be. He opened the door, naked, almost, with last night's shirt tied loincloth-style around him. He was heavy then, gone to seed fighterly, and the shirt was too small for the job it was asked to do. He'd just washed his hair, soapy water was dripping down his face, he hadn't got around to shaving. He didn't appear surprised that I'd outguessed his escape. He hugged me, we kissed, getting me wet. Yeah, he said, while I opened the bottle, yeah. Of course. It's just that road, isn't it. We all go down it. No bullshit. Some do. Some of us got return tickets. We'll have to flip for the glass. There's only one fucking glass. Yeah, I said. I filled it for him, hacked my own from the bottle. To this road, I said. A toast. To the storms to come, I said, and the storms coming after the storm. I was quoting Carl Sandburg, accurately. When I raised my glass to Joan, in her cheap bachelorette suite, I remembered the words and repeated them.

To the storm to come, I said.

You never seen a fucking storm, I thought, the stars coming after. You'll see fucking stars all right. There was a time you could look at them with your eyes open. As if he'd been listening, Devon said, you look at everything with your eyes closed.

Three walk-up stories above Skid Row. He'd taken the shirt—jesus, one of mine, I recognized it—off his middle and was lying face down on the bed, ass in the air, legs spread like tentacles, too stringy and loose to belong to the solid rest of him, one hand floorward bound, groping for the glass. I'm fucked, he said. I felt like a novelist, memorizing descriptions: his newly washed 25-carat hair against the rat-turd grey pillow. The dead end of last night's tomorrow outside, in the street; there is such a place folks, as The Street, and this is what it looks like. Devon, I said, Devon. Being fucked isn't good enough. You can't make it an excuse.

Self-righteous cocksucker.

I stayed with him, heaved and slept beside him, all that day, until sometime around dusk we got thrown out. I don't recall we did anything very interesting, sexually. When the manager crashed in, demanding only another night's payment, I had my nose in Devon's neck, my left hand cupping his uncertainly restless cock; he had a hand around my balls. I couldn't find my wallet. No matter, there wouldn't have been enough in it. We walked home.

You believe all that shit, Joan said. She stood up, framed herself in the comically asymmetric doorway to the closet kitchen. Don't you? Don't you?

THE NEW WORLD

ONE OF THE TIMES WE HAD MONEY, WE WENT TO San Francisco, Joan and I. This was before I knew Devon. I was cosmopolitan; I knew my way, perfectly, around the shining cities of the empire. I would take Joan out of her dank studio, into the weirdly transluminated Aegean light of San Francisco. It'll be good for your Vision, I think I said. On the train, Joan slept irritably, unconvinced by the adventure. I sat in the dome car, drinking bourbon, loving America for being only and exactly what it was: there. It shone for me, precisely, foreignly. America. I wanted to stumble down the train to Joan, wake her, slap her conscious, say look at it. Look, look. The New World! But I would have embarrassed myself, and her. The trees and grass and fences and farm shacks were, after all, basically the same as we have north of the border. No. Different. Joan, there's a life there, something like a history. You believe that? You believe all that shit. Let me sleep.

I must have let her sleep.

I won't forget this part. The most important things you get to see, Devon told me midway through one of my binges of screaming ideas at him, don't mean anything. To anybody else.

So shut up, will you. I doubt that I did. I let Joan sleep. The train rolled smoothly—I'd say majestically, if "rolled" weren't already bad enough—through a scenically banal countryside that had one great virtue to recommend it: it wasn't mine. Not one single stick, stone, weed, beast implicated me. There was a highway parallel to the tracks, and every car that raced up proclaimed its authority, its driver's birthwrit confidence in belonging where he was, on the road that links histories, the deaths they've taught us to love the naming of—Wait, Joan, wake up and wait, if I'm ever to know you please know me now.

The train south to California leaves very early in the morning; you get a not-bad sunrise for your trouble, if the weather's cooperative. An apocalyptic fifties liberal infusion of what else but light, over what else but the sea. And then . . . then it was as if . . . as if . . . as if I'd seen what the First Men had seen, when they woke to the world they'd soon lose forever, before you and I, Joan, Devon, were even so much as little crawly things in our parents' genitals, as if it loved us, loved the hope we represented, enough to make beauty especially for our use, this articulate sun somehow remembering to rise discreetly somewhere obscurely bypassing New York to gild Boston, wink at Patterson, en route to Pittsburgh and Cincinnati. At a truck stop in Toledo, Dave and Josie look up from their flapjacks, smile. Man, we gotta split. David always calls his women Man, it's got to do with dignity. Aboard the southbound train, I heard the riven voices: riding down into Salt Lake, I worried about where we'd get cigarettes, them Mormons don't smoke; the sun meanwhile, sailing west, made its fortune in Vegas and retired to . . . somewhere around L.A. The beach. It touched our hope, he's just murdered his wife or his father, take your choice, with the manicured fingers of mortality. Don Giannini smiled, as a man smiles who is a man. This is the earth of my heart, he said, we've lived it to its death; don't you know? I was looking into the face of a man twice my age, stout and landlord pink. If I voted for the wrong metaphor, he'd be president of your mother's republic. The shirt he wore dreamed of seeing Waikiki before it died. The pants had long since given up dreaming. They were content to hang there.

This was the beginning of the world. Kid Asher lay in his dim Canadian bed, illicit radio plugged to his dim Canadian ear: Bangor, Providence, Rochester, Buffalo. Call numbers the charm of which was that they didn't start with *C*. There was a mysterious call letter, *W*, which designated Another Place. There. Oh yeah, Joan said, when I tried to rouse her. You seen one tree you seen the fucken forest. Man. In case I forgot what sex I'd been.

I want my memory to preserve a world that has Joan in it.

The sun took a good look at L.A., and decided to die there. We were the world's destination. Buddy. It must've been Devon speaking. There was a point at which, somewhere in that afternoon, I had to take a piss. The can was down the hall, we decided. Follow your nose and you'll find it. I must have had to shit, I could have pissed in the sink. He lay back laughing while I wove down the hall, destination vague, trailing his sheet behind me.

When I got back I slid like a psychotic clam into bed beside him, sneaking a peek at my watch: four in the afternoon. He blazed. Every sinew gave off paragraphs I didn't want to translate; I was sleeping, wide awake, beside a magnificent foreign tongue. I think we sucked each other off, that day, maybe a couple of hours apart.

You believed him, Joan said. Devon. You still believe him.

Perhaps. What if I do?

By all the logic of liberation, Joan is the one who ought to get sympathetic treatment here. I sat in her wretched little suite thinking I'd like to be anywhere but there.

CODA

JOHNNY GIRARDI LEFT TOWN THE WAY HE'D COME into it, singing. But Johnny's song was driven away by wind and the ordinary racket, so that nobody, not even Asher, heard the words of it. For his heart's ease, he invented them:

May all our sins be forgiven
May our dreams be dreamed in vain.

Johnny'd never written anything like that. There was a time when Asher thought writing words would save him, from whence cometh salvation, he thinks now, to say it is to become free, what's that, to say it is to compel it to happen, and I alone am returned—wrecked my love and unequal to this world—to tell: I was never free, and always was nothing else but free, *may your indulgence* the magician said, though even then there was no indulgence, *set me free*; Johnny Girardi lifted up his voice and sang, *Duh-duh duh-duh duoodelly-doo*, and I, Asher, failed to hear the words out of his mouth, I knew the world was taking him back and he wanted to go, it still held a kind of promise for him. *No wonder* I thought as he said, clearly above the noise of the engines preparing to leave, I've killed too many of you already, fuck off while the fucking's good; then he raised a large dirty hand to hit or hold me, I had never seen anyone or anything more beautiful than he was then, I said *Go and tell the story, this one, this time, the way I'd tell it if I had the means.* I hadn't the means. The world was lost before I discovered it. What I could show you was shit, corruption, injustice, hatred, useless aspirations toward the passionate rape of garbage. I showed you that world, old buddy. I didn't want to tell you; now I give you the place in this mythology I'd have reserved for Devon, beautiful and good in the ancient and precise meaning of those words, he was beautiful enough that my cock screamed for him, good enough that every civil thought I had screamed for his mind's confirmation, I was so foolish, yet I give my love of him to you. There was no Devon. The simple ocean will stretch before me like an unfinished memory. Beautiful, I say, who must refuse beauty. Fuck, it's hard to do, I say. He was the property we'd all possess, could we reach so far, *hold me, I only want to be held*, our sins are not forgiven; I thought stupidly, I thought before I died he was coming in my direction, perfect, golden, a self-contained suite of the mind; but behind him there was the chorus line that wanted to kill my friends, kill him for the ordinary animal lust in him, the honest rage in him; I thought, I'm lucky to know truth and beauty at the same time; *Romantic*, you said, Petrov, while it was you who wanted yourself in my bed to prove something; I will not allow this—

Johnny Girardi took Asher to the train, southbound. They kissed on the platform, pretending not to care who watched. They didn't care, at that point. Johnny's bulk was large in Asher's arms, and he wished it were larger, to thrust him down into the muck he'd fled from. In all our mythologies, he thought, there's somebody who points the way, without whom we wouldn't go.

I said it, once, Asher said, for Devon. I won't say it again. Unless you ask me.

What was it?

He flew, he flew, before he died.

Let's pretend it was Joan, before she died. She saw our several bodies presented to her, objects of desire, the total of what she had to expect and hope for, the available, me, you, and all of us whose love was so small and cheap, so easy in a world where easiness was taken for granted, you could fuck anything that moved and did—

You broke me, broke my fucking heart, I don't know why.

They've come to get Devon, and I stand in the doorway, denying knowledge. Next year they'll come to get us. A long time from now, I'll approach that ocean, see Devon, want and refuse him as I've wanted and refused every possibility of love that's tempted me. So much for history. In the nation of my birth, idiocy assumes the guise of power. Asher, weary after long days, speaks in his soft frightened voice of beauty and truth, a better world than the one he's stuck with, things I won't admit to the meaning of, though he says through his crazy eyes, *This is all we have, all we know, this is the grace given us before the crunch comes down, meanwhile I deny everything.*

He has the tickets in his sleazy Sally Ann coat. The way out.

He's whispering so loud you could hear him the other side of the river.

Go, he says. Tell the story.

He called a cab, to take us to the train. He'd bought the tickets, made the reservations, committed the necessary crimes. He'd consulted no one.

It was one of those mornings that accuse us with their perfection, the sky looking like the poem you flunked for forgetting the words of, the trees green like house plants desperate for less than fatuous conversation. The perfect world was trying to manifest itself, and failing. I held you briefly and said, It's all right, the best of our friends are dead and the rest don't give a shit. It appalled me how cheap our truths had become. We ate porridge, oatmeal, and week-old hot dogs that stank worse cooked than frozen. I didn't mind, and didn't die.

Go, Asher said. Go now.

Let's end now. Let's be quiet. I want to turn my heart, Asher said, I want to turn it now to the death of the world. You, he said to me, you tell it if it can be told. I didn't know what he meant. Tell them, he said, tell the assholes what really happened, what it was like. That can't be done, I said, I'm sorry. Don't spend your whole fucking life apologizing, he said. We were alive once. And while we were we made mistakes, I said. I couldn't look at him, the face I'd held and formed like foam was one I'd never looked at and couldn't now, let's *end,* I thought, let's be quiet, but he struggled in my thick arms and said, The last words should be yours, and for his sake they are.

THE LIFE OF THE MIND

TO ANYBODY WHO PRESUMES TO LIVE IT, OR WHO tries to, the life of the mind must at times present itself as no less mysterious than any other species of life might appear to an alien observer. For the famous prescription of Dr. Williams, *no ideas but in things*, substitute the converse, and tremble. Then double the peril for the writer of mere fiction, for whom the world of sensible objects, events, persons, the world of actual Being, is often darker and stranger than its other side. He wakes cursing himself for having forgotten his dreams; passes the day cursing his friends for inviting stray reality into his reconstruction of those dreams; and at length falls asleep again cursing the frailty of Creation which neglected to provide his subconscious with an electric typewriter and another bottle of whisky. Somewhere in the process, a quantum of loss can be taken for granted.

Among the self-declared writers of his generation, some whom are still alive and in print, Asher was chiefly remarkable for the infrequency and unimportance of his publications. His entire bibliography could be inscribed, with room to spare, on the back of a postcard. Contemporary scholarship continues to ignore him as significantly as it did in his lifetime; and in fairness it must be said that this is not altogether a case of wilful neglect or, indeed, professional jealousy, as a handful of simple-minded commentators have intimated. Asher was, of course, personally and intellectually unattractive to his peers. Mild and ineffectual in manner, as well, and pathologically shy of self-promotion, he possessed that quality of ingrown elitism which, thinking itself unduly harassed by the vulgar world, withdraws into nonentity. Not surprisingly, then, his work demanded to be misunderstood, and so it was, and is.

In the circumstances, it may well be wondered why I trouble myself to revive a reputation which hardly existed in the first place. A bad conscience may be counted an acceptable motive for good works, but not necessarily for literary exhumation. I cannot deny that I am, with this project, attempting to purge a private guilt of my own: it is no secret that such formal education as I have I owe largely to Gus Asher's anachronistic insistence that I obtain it, or that having done so I immediately used it to free myself from his influence and to secure exactly that comfortable style of life which he had repudiated. Unless I am sorely mistaken, Asher was certainly aware of what he was embarking upon when he embarked upon me, and it is perhaps not reprehensible that in the course of things I set sail for a calmer anchorage than he.

Nonetheless, he himself forgave me readily enough. He was so addicted to forgiveness that he trafficked in it not unlike the medieval Church with its Indulgences: since the full catalogue of sin was available to his imagination, all of it was pardonable in advance. What I came to appreciate, later, was that the very idea of sin was *comic* to him: morality as such was an entertainment, a masque, at which he sat bemused, slightly drunk, in the Royal Box.

In any transcription, meanings must be guessed at, words rescued by airlift from the wastes of incoherence, punctuation imposed like foreign laws upon a conquered tribe. A charitable view, to which I am occasionally tempted to subscribe, holds that Asher thought musically, or rather, *orchestrally*; but he was either too stubborn or too lazy to learn a correct notation, so that the sounds in his head might be performable in concert by an intelligence other than his own. He was, as he admitted to me, essentially a soliloquist, and in this eccentricity he was paradoxically at odds with the sentimental anarcho-communism and neo-Romantic idealism he liked to espouse, in public, as an impossible antidote to the complacent rhetoric of everybody else. He frequently dissolved conversations merely by murmuring that he had no desire to be right: that it suited him much better to be wrong. The core of the Real, he said, was resistance; then, typically, he revised himself and argued that what he had meant to say was that the core of the Real is resistant to the corrosion of thought, as it is to the balm of error. He had in such moments an aspect of ferocious loneliness, which made the gregarious yearn to strike him.

To approach his writing through anecdote is to disservice him; but to enter through the mechanics of scholarship is to betray him. No character in the most explicit of his explicit stories resembles more than haphazardly any specific individual: resemblances are always imputed; incidents recalled as fact long after they had failed to occur; biography is a maze in which a reader will die of loneliness sooner than starvation. Asher held memory hostage to desire, in a low period when neither was adequate to experience. A tour of his personal history yields little insight: it is an official visit to an exploded coal-mine, or any industrial disaster, where the object of the ceremony is not to see what is there, but to be recorded as having been seen seeing it and weeping. In the only letter I received from him after his disappearance, he instructed me to finish the book he had begun, however I chose to finish it, because *the sole object of my art is continuity, that the beat go on . . . .*

To me, in the early days, Asher's concerns were laughable, as in his calmer moods, they were to him. Who could desire more than to be fucked, fed, drugged? He had been all of those. Into the sorry chronicle of his days I make my entrance; of the life he wrote about, I remember nothing because I was not present. In the last weeks, he seemed to be writing about me, or some dreamed-of creature he thought I was, and I cannot identify myself in the portrait: I always wanted what he despised, because I had never had it nor the opportunity to seize it, and he had refused it. He sweated and wept, trying to tell me; he slept when I was awake; he stared at photographs of exotic places, read maps of unvisited cities as a Cabalist reads the sacred ciphers. He wearied me. There was in him an unkindness which gave the lie to his charade of generosity;

elaborately, he gave his friends the means to kill him if and whenever they chose. The sole return he could offer them was to write about them, obscurely, when he supposed their attention was deployed elsewhere. And nobody, plumbling the pages he plumbled (a word, incalculably descriptive, which he blamed on his typography), could discern the focus of his attention.

Literary history will contemn these reflections as the apologetics of a used-up Impressionist; which I daresay they are, and I am. Asher had no use for the saccharine reflection of the blurred image, and no strength to paint the sharp one; I repeat "reflections" here because it describes the least lovable aspect of his thought, which, like a mirror aimed nastily toward the sun, burned rank little holes in the carpets and upholstery of his friends' lives. The Impressionists blinkered the sight of things with the pale murk of love, an affection for the visible qua its visibility; Asher, who at his most competent had difficulty negotiating a city crosswalk, loved murk, precisely for its blinkering faculty, irrespective of whatever was on hand to be blinkered.

The lurid tale of Asher and Devon and Joan and Eli, et al., evidently has no foundation in its author's memory: the murder on which it is predicated is not mentioned in the records of local crime; the opera from which it purportedly derives can be heard in no twentieth-century repertory. Those of us who knew Asher were familiar with his fear of literary invention; he genuinely believed that if he wrote about a fictitious occurrence, some approximation of it was bound to take place in "real" life. To write as his imagination decreed, therefore, he felt compelled to offer himself up, in his own name, as an authorial sacrifice. If he died in the plot, nobody else would have to. Paradoxically, if he killed *everybody* off, the few he cherished might, to confound him, live.

This frame of mind, verging as it did on the lunatic, perplexed those of his readers whom it did not alienate outright. It had no metaphysical illogic to defend it, no psychological rhetoric to soften it, no solid politics to sustain it. It could be apprehended, if at all, as a hermit's interior dialogue with himself, isolation having frozen away the tune of other human voices; toward what we think of as the end, it has the monochromatic insistence of those elderly inebriates who whisper and orate to themselves in rundown bars like the ones Asher haunted; it so far excluded art that Asher, having abolished himself as an artist, had little choice but to do likewise as a man. Perhaps intentionally, perhaps not, he had perfected a structure the one conceivable occupation of which was its own extinction.

Rude opinions have been given as to why I, of all people, should have been vouchsafed custody of his archive. The simple reason is naturally the one least agreeable to scholarship: nobody else happened to want the stuff. I similarly attained custody of his debts, his quarrels, and a trunkload of rank clothes. The notion of custodianship imparts a value to the things taken into one's charge, but Asher's leavings were without anything like extrinsic value: I had them because they were left behind and I lacked the heartlessness to throw them out. Indeed, there was no Out to throw them into. I emptied the ashtrays into other ashtrays, emptied the garbage into the fireplace, lit the fire, sat back and drank the last of his liquor; a woman from the University came to visit; I do not recall that we talked about Asher at all. His disappearance was as definitive as his writing was not. The rooms in which he had composed his stories bore no trace of him, beyond an odour of decaying underwear and old socks, beyond scraps of crumpled notepaper flushed under the bed, beyond a thin vapour leaking from the cardboard cartons in which he'd piled those few of his writings which were to survive him.

Asher's account of our first encounter, and friendship thereafter, is passably accurate; of our parting it is fanciful; of the time between it prudently says nothing. He compresses into a vest-pocketful of allusions a mythology which means vastly more to him than it ever did to me, and I truly do know at which points he is referring to me, at which to a fabulous creature of his dreaming, at which to himself. So far as can be determined, the mighty fiction of which he thought himself capable was never written down, or only in fragments, and it is beyond my competence to say what end he expected it to meet. He sent me to school so that I might not follow in his path, and condemned me to edit him, to rewrite him, so that I would do just that. Now it scarcely matters. The work is done, to whatever purpose, and I am tired.

Johnny Girardi left town the way he came into it, singing.

—J. Girardi, Vancouver, 198–

EDITOR'S NOTE

YOU AREN'T SUPPOSED TO BE READING THIS BOOK

... as I'm not supposed to be ploughing through the box of Fraser's papers like a scavenger at the dump. Every so often I scream, "Enough, Fraser. Get on with it!" Were all this stuff truly mine I'd grab a handful of variously tinted manuscripts and throw them in no particular direction.

But Fraser didn't ask me to do this, would have hated it, was always skittish about people seeing things before he thought they were finished. Since he seldom thought anything was finished (finished equating with perfect) we saw little beyond the two thin volumes of fiction published during his life. There were rumours of masterworks in progress referred to as "The Great Beast," "Ceremonies of the Horseman," "The Canadian Book of the Dead ... " but nobody saw them, or very much of them. Was anybody prepared for the actual quantity of material?

Well, I guess there were harbingers. The stucco grotto/safe-house in Dunbar, for example. Shortly after Fraser began to occupy it, the patina had already been laid down: a fairly ordinary illegal student suite was becoming Fraser's Place, furnished in large measure with beer cases. No kidding, the coffee table was a door, or something, on stacks of cases of beer bottles, mostly Labatt's 50. (A measure of the scope of things: in the days when beer bottles were redeemable at two-bits a dozen we took back sixty-three bucks' worth.)

During one of Fraser's late-sixties pilgrimages to Glace Bay, someone said, "Let's clean up Dondel's place for him." This kind of energy is inexorable. That may have been when the $63 worth of beer bottles got taken to the depot, when the walls were scrubbed for the last time, when the victims of somebody's judgement of extraneous papers got shoved into green garbage bags, when the hulls of countless Sportsman filter cigarette packages . . . "Wait a minute!" Somebody (Janet always claimed it was she) said, "these all have writing on them." Sure enough, each package had been disemboweled, turned inside out, and covered with a tiny amount of prose fiction in Fraser's absolutely elementary-school teacher legible hand. Further rapid research determined that other papers maybe were important too, but (remember, this was a cleaning frenzy) not enough to interfere with the project. The compromise (Janet, again) was to put all the papers with writing on them into their own series of garbage bags which Dondel could throw out, or not, once his gratitude had dissipated.

Dondel, of course, was furious, as he always was when someone tried to Improve His Life for him. But he did come to terms with those garbage bags and kept them for years (not excepting the ones that actually contained garbage). They became an aleatory filing system. On the rare occasions when he wanted to show us something in progress, he could burrow into the correct bag and nearly always come up with the right cigarette pack.

When I was asked to edit Fraser's stuff I envisaged being handed the nearly twenty years' accumulation of garbage bags and cigarette packages. But no. Although he had continued to write on anything handy (or not so) in a script that deteriorated to the point of final indecipherability, someone had been through things and typed out most of what there was.

One of the few times the two of us discussed the nuts and bolts of writing, ink-on-paper issues, we discovered we were both into pages. Pages as structural units. He liked to get them perfect; I liked to get them finished. Later we both adopted the endless rolls of newsprint favoured by Pulp Press, and later still, word processors, although Fraser and the word processor approached each other with incipient animosity. What did that do to our sense of structure?

Fraser on nuts and bolts: "One goes pootling off to the local store and buys a 'Mammoth' scribbler . . ." Yup, there it is in the box, some of the pages have writing on them, many don't. Interleaved are other papers, handbills, letterheads, all with Fraser's handwriting on the back, or any other clear spaces. There are a dozen or so similar scribblers, ring binders, three-subject notebooks. Surprising then that none of them was apparent in the apartment amid the stacks of *Georgia Straights* and *New Yorkers*, pamphlets, posters, tracts.

He couldn't tolerate a mistake on a page, would tear one out for nothing more serious than a typo and start the page over; if one word wasn't appropriate, start the page over; any advanced versions, start over: the quest for the perfect page. But Fraser, you could have thrown out the imperfect ones! Or at least given some indication which version came closest, which last.

After a time it begins to seem that each balky page was meant to be included. In *Ignorant Armies* the narrator refers to the dozen or one thousand pages that begin "Johnny Girardi came into town singing . . ." There are more than twenty-five, fewer than a thousand. So I've left you with several.

Presuming I received my mandate from Fraser as Girardi received his from Asher—"Finish it . . . write it off"—I began with the assumption that he wouldn't have died before *Ignorant Armies* was finished, an illusion that lasted nearly until the end of the carton. But none of us, reader or editor, was supposed to be reading the stuff. Even in the approach to actual publication, Fraser's "final" version would be snatched back for revision. When he typeset his own work it was revised in the Compugraphic, was not even safe from its creator on the paste-up table. Nor did publication mean it was "finished."

In the box I found a letter he wrote to me twenty years ago and never mailed. It was nearly devoid of content *qua* letter but contained some stuff germinal to the novels. I had been searching for a message from various recently dead people in my life but this wasn't it. It was among Janet's stuff—feeling then, too, like an intruder, going through her papers after she died, looking for her message to me—that I may have found it: a Sportsman package covered with that unmistakable handwriting. I remember it turning up after he'd stayed with us in St. Catharines. I imagine he'd accidentally left it for her to find and she (accidentally) for me.

> *People are not diminished by what is said of them—or what use is made of them by those who are lesser in being, or by what they are led to do—someone is—himself, entire—and that is all, finally, that can be said of him. Then, nothing done by another, or to another should greatly dismay us; it is the being, the totality, that we have accepted, that we love—and we cannot say we love at all unless we love his freedom, his capacity for absurdity and for inflicting pain, his responses, his choices. The wholeness of a being includes what we cannot know—the potential. Genuinely to love is to accept the limitations of our own knowledge, our own understanding, the smallness of our power in another's life . . . to accept these things, and yet love, and take on without regret the consequences we cannot foresee. Anything less is destructive, a false diminishing (in the mind) of a given reality. Love transcends any situation—it is all situations.*
>
> —JBC, HALFMOON BAY, B.C.

Dedication

If this book is mine to dedicate, it is for Viola Fraser, Kenneth Caple, June Enright, Rosemary Hollingshead, and all parents who have had strange and gifted offspring die before them.

Acknowledgement

Ignorant Armies could not have leapt into its final form without the welcome input of Brian Lam, Steve Osborne, and Mary Schendlinger.